River Liffey

Trinity College

Merrion Square

Pembroke Street

Upper Mount Street

Herbert Place

Image overleaf (and on last page): view of Dublin *c.* 1850.
Back cover image: from Baldwin & Cradock map of Dublin, 1836.

Behind a Georgian Door

...At the front she looked on out on the canal's
prettiest feature—lovely little Huband Bridge...

Behind a Georgian Door

Perfect Rooms, Imperfect Lives

by

Artemesia D'Ecca

PHÆTON
PUBLISHING LTD.
—— Dublin ——

Behind a Georgian Door

FIRST PUBLISHED IN IRELAND & U.K. 2016
by Phaeton Publishing Limited, Dublin

Copyright © Artemesia D'Ecca, 2016

Artemesia D'Ecca has asserted her right
to be identified as the author of this work

Cover, illustrations, & design copyright ©
O'Dwyer & Jones Design Partnership, 2016

Printed and bound in U.K. and in U.S.A.

*British Library Cataloguing In Publication
Data: a catalogue record for this book
is available from the British Library*

ISBN: 978-1-908420-15-2   HARDBACK
ISBN: 978-1-908420-14-5   PAPERBACK

The places and the historic events and historic figures in
this book are real, but the stories are works of fiction: any
resemblance of the fictional characters to persons living
or dead is entirely coincidental.

Contents

...'I just wish it had a better history,' she said, staring down at the Georgian street vista. 'It's such a secret view and so undisturbed—if only it hadn't been built on all that misery'...

Christmas 2013

HERBERT PLACE

I HAD A HOT SHOWER in the peach-coloured marble bathroom with the built-in television at the foot of the giant bath, and then Martin had a tepid one. There was a rule – Martin's – that the hot water would be turned on for half an hour in the morning and twenty minutes in the evening – never in between and never for longer. So I always got up early to have my shower first, and then went back to bed with Reggie and the dog. The house was unheated, but once I put on my cashmere bathrobe – another relic, like the glittering bathroom, of the far-away world before The Crash – and put a cap and a cardigan on Reggie, we were comfortable enough. When we pulled the goose-down quilt up to our chins, and Chauncey, the border collie, settled himself at our feet, we were in the warmest spot in the house. I used to spend the time reading to Reggie, and she was building a vocabulary that startled even me. Fond of long words, she would occasionally, and by sheer chance, throw one out with something close to accuracy.

'You're expostulating,' she had said suddenly the evening before when Martin was talking away heatedly – normal for him these days – about the new property tax which we hadn't a hope of paying. I hadn't even realized Reggie was listening to him. I certainly wasn't.

The interruption silenced Martin in mid-sentence, and both of us began to laugh, joined almost immediately by a bewildered but willing Reggie. None of which sounds too remarkable, but in the climate of dour edginess in which we had got used to spending our days, it was a memorable enough moment. The sight of the three of us laughing together was one that vast, freezing, flag-stoned kitchen with four sinks, newly excavated wine cellar, and three cooking areas had rarely witnessed in its refurbished lifetime.

Until that happened, the day had been the grimmest one yet.

Martin had been at a funeral in the morning. I should have been there too, but instead I'd stayed in bed until the afternoon and let Reggie watch television – a big treat for her. I had said nothing to Reggie about the funeral. She knew and liked the man who was being buried – sweet Joe Dunne, the contractor who had done the renovation of the house for us – and she would be full of talk and questions that I'd sooner not hear.

The way he died was awful – although for young men in the building trade, it was a manner of death that had become creepily predictable since 2008. He had crashed at speed, alone in his van, into a wall in the small hours of the morning. Two other contractors we knew had died the same way.

I'd gone to both of those funerals, and they had been bad, but this one I just couldn't cope with. I really *knew* Joe. I'd even known his little boy, Luke, since he was three. Joe had come to the house one Sunday to do an emergency repair after slates blew off in a storm, and he had brought Luke – proudly – along with him.

Back then, before Reggie, I didn't have much time for toddlers, but Luke was different – the gentlest little boy I'd ever seen. Chauncey was a rambunctious new puppy at the time, but Luke was so peaceful that even wild Chauncey quietened when he sat beside him. While his father and Martin went up to the roof, Luke stayed with me, and I started racking my brain for some treat I could give him – we kept a bare cupboard in those pre-Reggie days, when we hardly ever ate at home. 'Would you like a piece of buttery toast?' I asked finally, remembering the half loaf of bread I'd seen in the freezer. 'With strawberry jam?'

Luke nodded, and I did a slice for each of us. Luke shared his slice with Chauncey, while I put in a DVD of *Lady and the Tramp*. I stretched out at one end of the sofa, and he and Chauncey snuggled together at the other; Luke and I watched it and Chauncey slept. Then – I suppose because it was all just so damn relaxing – I fell asleep too. And so, apparently, did Luke, because the next thing I knew, a frightened-looking Martin was shaking us all awake. 'God, I thought there had been a gas leak or something. You all looked unconscious.'

The last time I met Joe and Luke was the previous Christmas. We had run into one another at the hardware shop in Ranelagh. My mother had asked me to find a replacement string of lights for one that wasn't working, and Joe and Luke were on the same errand. The cheaper lights – the ones I was looking for – seemed to have been sold. I got the impression those were the ones Joe was looking for as well. Neither of us admitted anything, but we both went home empty-handed.

I had suspected Joe was hit even worse by the crash than we were, but I never knew for sure until I saw his house up for sale over the summer in one of those repossession auctions. It was a big old house in Rathmines that he had bought to renovate. Martin was shaken when he heard. He tried to find out where Joe and his family were living, but no one seemed to know. It was only after Joe's death that we learned they had moved in with his wife's mother.

Today, Martin was going out on his own again – this time to another of those international jobs fairs which had been cropping up in Dublin regularly since the crash – although maybe a little less often now than before – now that the economy was supposed to be improving. I imagine it *was* improving for some. I mean, the unemployment lines surely *had* to be going down, with every youngster we knew hopping it to London or New York or Sydney or Vancouver.

Anyway, Martin never missed a fair. He was a structural engineer – a really good one too. Ireland didn't want that profession at the moment, but it seemed that other countries still did. Canada, in particular. Recruiters from Australia and the Middle East would be at the jobs fair too, but Canada, at the moment, was the favoured destination for the newly poor of the building game.

At least half-a-dozen couples we knew, most of whom Martin had worked with – architects, engineers, quantity surveyors, interior designers – had gone to British Columbia already and were managing, although most of them found it a hard grind. Even when they were earning a decent salary, their assets, for the most part, had vanished with the Irish crash, and at best they were starting over again when they were older, tireder, had families to support, and had been softened by an easy life. The ones who had any thoughts of coming home again – and who cared about their credit rating when they did – were worst off, as most of them were paying back debts on Irish properties the banks had already repossessed. The ones who never wanted to see Ireland again didn't have that problem at least. They could ignore the banks' letters. They were the lucky ones, I often thought.

'We can't keep putting it off,' Martin said, when he was pressing me to go with him. 'Unless I can get one of those Canada jobs now – *and* we start getting a big rent for the house as well – the bank won't even think about renegotiating with us, and the house is gone. What the hell are we going to do then?'

This was talk I was tired of hearing and didn't want Reggie to hear at all. I scowled at him.

'You remember Tommy, don't you,' he went on, not noticing. 'The red-headed guy from Roscommon – the one Chauncey liked. He did the services for that last building I did on the quays. Well, he came back for the funeral.'

'All the way from British Columbia?' I said guiltily.

'He's got a second job there now – half a second job anyway. I don't think it's full time. It may not even be that legit, but it sounds like he's earning real money. He was saying I'd be able to do the same. And you'd be earning something too. You mightn't be editing magazines straightaway, but you'd be making something.'

I had heard all of this – or something very similar – before. When he finished, I said that I didn't want to go to the recruitment fair. That was all I said. I gave no explanation. We had stopped being polite to one another. When we spoke at all these days, it was usually to fling insults or to make points, although knowing how much that upset Reggie, we tried not to do it in front of her – or in front of Chauncey either, one of nature's peacemakers. On hearing a sharp tone or a raised voice, Chauncey's policy – an effective one – was to try to poke his nose into the offending mouth to silence it.

I sort of knew how big our debt was but didn't like to think about it, and I'd stopped months ago looking at the statements and letters. I'd stopped answering the phone, too, because the debt collectors were ringing us daily now. So maybe we did have to decide soon between a nasty Irish bankruptcy – God, if only we could go for an easy English one, like the really rich did – and being owned by the bank forever, but anyone would go mad thinking too much about that sort of thing, it seemed to me, and certainly Martin and I were beyond the point of drawing any comfort from one another. He told me I didn't take it all seriously enough. I told him his sense of humour had vanished with our credit rating. Alone in the house with Reggie and Chauncey, I couldn't stop singing that old Tennessee Ernie Ford song about owing your soul to the company store. I never sang it in front of Martin though.

For a while, I used to complain about him to my parents, but all they ever said was, 'Ah, poor Martin,' or something equally annoying; so then I had to stop talking about him altogether, which meant I was mad at them too as often as not, and that didn't help much.

I looked forward now to the days I had to myself. I never hung around the house any more if I could avoid it. Not only did every inch of that millstone depress me, it was also just too damn cold. The single radiator that was ever turned on any more was the one in Reggie's bedroom on cold nights. Our only other heating came from a fire we lit, late in the day, in the small basement room leading off the kitchen, which, luckily, we had set up as a space for an au pair, with its own small bathroom. That was where Reggie had her bath in the evenings.

I often thought how nice it would be if we could turn that tiny, semi-warm room into a bedroom for the three of us, but we had spent so much money fixing up the lavish bedrooms at the top of the house that Martin was determined we get the use out of them. Fine for him I thought to myself every night as we made the freezing trudge up to the top floor. He didn't feel the cold, but it was November now, and I was perished all the time.

Today, as soon as he was gone, I planned to take Reggie and Chauncey out with me, and we would stop at some café where Reggie would have hot chocolate and I would have coffee – all of which amounted to a big secret sin now. In the old days – during the boom and before Reggie – Martin and I hardly ever ate at home. Maybe it was the memory of all the money we wasted back then that had Martin bothered now. Dublin's restaurants were always bad value, but during the boom... One night we came back from a dinner out and were watching an old movie on television, a comedy western in which James Garner was having a meal at some sort of gold-rush town, and between the time he sat down and the time he finished eating, the price of the meal had gone up. 'Dublin,' we both shouted at the screen.

I didn't pay for the little outings with Reggie from our joint account. When Reggie told Martin about the hot chocolate and he asked how I had paid, I said my mother had given me the money. I wasn't going to admit to Martin that I had started selling some of my own things – mainly the clothes I had bought in my throwing-money-around days that still hadn't gone out of fashion: so far, two coats and four jackets and two Gucci bags. Of course, the clothes were pretty old by this – none of them bought since 2008 – but luckily, I was more conservative than even my mother when it came to buying coats. I avoided fashion, bought good labels, and expected them to last about ten years. The woman at Clothes Ex loved my stuff and gave me a decent price; the really fashionable might think them tired, but then the really fashionable weren't likely to be shopping at Clothes Ex.

Because of Chauncey, we were never able to retreat to the inside snugness of a café on these expeditions, but always ended up outdoors with the smokers, where dogs were allowed. I would bring colouring books for Reggie, nab a table near a heater, and while Reggie worked away happily with her crayons, I would think about money and indulge in dark thoughts – something I avoided doing at home.

In the house, I kept my thinking in check: hate, fury, grief, fantasies of revenge were not things I wanted bouncing off the walls for Reggie to pick up; but sitting on the pavement of a busy street in a haze of smokers and traffic and with Reggie distracted, I thought whatever I wanted; and most of it wasn't too pretty.

This outing started well. Our destination was Camden Street, which meant that we could go by the canal for most of the way. It was a fair distance for Reggie, but one collateral benefit of our troubles was that Reggie had got very fit. I took her on these long walks every day the weather allowed – it kept me from fighting with Martin when he was at home, or from comfort-eating if I was alone. Reggie loved the outings, and had developed the stamina of a pre-motorcar farm child.

Chauncey was never easy with traffic, but he enjoyed the grassy path along the canal. There were a few places where we often stopped. Between Baggot Street and Leeson Street bridges, the bench with the bronze figure of Patrick Kavanagh had taken Reggie's fancy from the time she was being wheeled past it in her buggy, and she always wanted us to sit beside him for a minute. Beside Charlemont Street Bridge, there were the now glorious willow trees. When I was young, I had hardly noticed these trees, but in the years I wasn't looking, they had grown to be a sight to stare at. The last time we passed, someone had hung a swing from one of them. Two little girls were taking turns sitting on it, and Reggie dragged on my hand as she looked back at them enviously.

South Richmond Street, Chauncey didn't care for much, but he and I both thought it was better than it used to be. To a motorist, it still looked much as it always did – windswept and God-forsaken, except for Christy Bird's overflowing old-furniture shop – but to a wandering pedestrian, it now could seem almost exotic in parts – a bit like the street of a down-at-heel port city in a film noir. Buildings that had been derelict – or at least looked derelict – hosted interesting little enterprises, some of them with hints of Africa and the East. The smoking ban helped – a surprising number of tiny cafés had appeared, all of them with at least a single table outside. When an ambulance with a siren went by, Chauncey tried to ensconce himself under one of the tables, but I pulled him on, wanting to get my errand out of the way before we treated ourselves.

The errand was for my neighbours, Helen and Mary,

who lived in a flat a few houses down. They were getting a new window blind for their kitchen from a shop in Camden Street, and they wanted to hear my formerly-the-editor-of-a-design-magazine opinion on their colour choice before they committed themselves. We had nearly reached the shop and I was fishing around in my new, five-euro, crossbody bag for a paint chart when Reggie squealed and gave a ferocious tug at my sleeve. 'Mummy, look,' she said excitedly. I did look, and then something happened to me which I still can't explain.

At the time, I even wondered was it a heart attack or a stroke or something, but it wasn't, thank heaven. 'Probably stress,' I was told when I asked about it later, although it must have been pretty extreme stress. For a second or two, I was so unsure of being able to stay on my feet that I had to lean against the wall of the shop for support.

With hindsight, I was inclined to put the episode down to one of those straw-landing-on-a-camel's-back moments; but at the time, it was a total mystery. There I was, hardly a thought in my head, and facing nothing more demanding than the familiar prospect of matching a fabric sample to a paint colour, when suddenly – although nothing had happened except that quick glance down the street – all I could think was what on earth was the point of carrying on. The feeling of despair was almost overpowering – as if for one second, the blinkers I had been wearing to get through the days had slipped, and I was seeing the world maybe as Martin saw it. In that moment, I couldn't even imagine how we'd be able to keep going.

When it passed, the idea of mulling over the tone of a window blind was beyond me, but I didn't want to go home. Anyway, if I were going to have a heart attack, a busy street might be a better place for it than an empty house. At least there would be plenty of people to mind Reggie and Chauncey, both of whom, at the moment, were pulling me forward with all their might which, in Chauncey's case, was quite a lot.

Camden Street didn't excite them generally – they enjoyed the fruit and vegetable stalls all right, but they were used to them. Today, however, a mammoth Christmas delivery was underway, and apples, oranges, carrots, and Brussels sprouts had almost vanished under mounds of mistletoe and holly. The quantity of greenery was unusual – it looked as if a month of Christmas deliveries had been made at the one time. There was a bit of pavement visible, but most of it had vanished under Christmas trees in nets.

I had to struggle to hold on to the two of them. Chauncey was straining – with some success – to have a sniff at every trunk and Reggie was dancing between me and Chauncey, talking nonstop to us both. Putting an arm around Chauncey, she even took a leaf from his book and sniffed the still-netted branches.

When we finally got clear of the stalls, I collapsed at the first café that had a working outdoor heater and that looked like it could put a glass of wine in my hand. I ordered a hot chocolate for Reggie, and decided, in all the circumstances, to order a glass of Champagne for myself. I didn't give the order verbally to the waiter though, but held up the menu and pointed to what I wanted. When he brought the glass, I told Reggie it was soda – it wasn't going to serve any purpose for Martin to get wind of this particular indulgence. The Champagne was poor stuff, sweet and with a bit of an undertaste, but it helped all the same. I remember hearing once that the Army used to keep small bottles of Champagne for soldiers when they were sick. That was a good idea, I think.

I had a few colouring books for Reggie in my bag – giveaway ones that had been handed out at the supermarket as a Christmas promotion. I set her up with these and with a packet of crayons, and she got to work contentedly while I, as usual, did arithmetic in my head. Unfortunately, nothing ever made the figures improve. They always added up to the same total, which might have been translated into words as: you're screwed, and it doesn't matter how much you scrimp. That was the real problem. It was what I understood and Martin didn't, it seemed to me. There was nothing we could do that mattered. If we could make a difference to the debt by going on living in the miserable way we were living, I wouldn't have minded doing without – well, I could have tolerated it better anyway – but we were making no difference.

Our biggest problem – as for everyone – was The Mortgage. We had to pay back nearly €10,000 a month, and now we were way behind in payments. I had no idea how much we owed at this stage. I think Martin didn't either – even he couldn't bear to open the envelopes any more. The price of houses like ours – big ones near the city centre and fixed up to the nines – had started to rise again slowly after the big drop, but it was still worth less than half what we'd spent on it.

The last year we had real work was 2008, but even then Martin hadn't been paid for most of what he did. That was the start of our problems. If he had been paid for that year, we might have kept our heads above water, but once the arrears started climbing we had no hope of catching up – like everyone else in the same mess.

I suppose it didn't help that both of us had been working for the same untouchable rich man – a developer, of course, but also a publisher, and worst of all, a sort of financial guru to Dublin's well-connected. OK, before the money dried up, we thought he was all right. He had put Martin in charge of some of his biggest projects, and it was because of Martin that he had given me the job of editing his design magazine – an over-priced, shiny thing that had been taken off life-support when the crash came. At least my salary had been paid up to date when that happened, but it wasn't a big salary. Martin was the serious earner, and he owed Martin – disastrously – a small fortune. Like others of the filthy rich, he somehow managed to declare bankruptcy in England, which allowed him to be back in business in just a year. He returned to Ireland then, and when we heard on the news that he was to be added to the list of former moguls who were to be put on a salary of €200,000 by the new government agency set up after the crash – he was to be a sort of consultant – Martin pressed him for some money. That was a big mistake. Martin got no money, and they fell out permanently.

For a while, we had been able to live off savings. After they ran out – which didn't take long – we sold the few shares we had, although they weren't really worth anything after the crash. Then we sold some paintings and some antique rugs we had bought in the good times but their value had collapsed too. Surprisingly soon, there seemed to be nothing left.

Like everyone else in the same mess, we thought at first that we could give the keys of the house back to the bank, write off what we'd lost, and start over. Apparently you could do that in most places, but in Ireland the bank could chase us forever for the difference between the value of the house and the ever-growing amount owed on it. Not many had known that before the crash; now everyone knew it. If we declared bankruptcy, we would be twelve years as bankrupts. They were talking about changing that law, all right – maybe as soon as next year – and bringing the time down to three years, and making it cheaper; but that hadn't happened yet, and anyway, even three years was a long time in Reggie's life.

My idea was that we should just 'disappear' – I'd read online about a lot of people our age who were doing that; we could post the keys of the house to the bank, leave the country, and then vanish from the bank's sight until maybe it couldn't chase us for the debt anymore.

I thought we should at least look into the idea of disappearing, but somewhere in Europe, so that Reggie wouldn't lose touch with her grandparents. Martin said the idea was mad.

His preferred idea, as I summed it up for him, was that we'd work ourselves ragged in British Columbia so that we could be in debt forever in Ireland just to keep the stupid house. And he didn't think that was mad? Every time I raised the idea of simply abandoning Herbert Place – and the fortune we had spent there – our quarrels got nastier.

'You're the one who wanted it,' he pointed out sourly whenever the subject arose. 'You're the one who decided we had to buy that house no matter what.'

'And you are a tiresome pain,' I snapped back. 'As if the suburban eyesore you'd have had us buy would have kept its value.'

That was as elevated as our conversations got these days.

It didn't help that he was right about some things. Maybe I had got us more into debt than necessary because I so badly wanted just one type of house – a four or five-storey Georgian inside the canals. Not that those places were always the most expensive houses, but the square footage to be fixed up in them never failed to add up. I'd looked at every tall Georgian that came up on both sides of the Liffey, but when one came available in Herbert Place, I pounced immediately. I knew it wasn't the purest of Georgian streets – a dry-bags who came to our housewarming pointedly reminded me of this when he said he *supposed* we could *get away* with calling it Georgian as the land to build it on had been acquired in 1830, but of course we knew didn't we that the house itself hadn't been put up until 1832?

'Which is why it's so solidly built, I suppose,' I had answered, vowing never to invite him around again.

I had personal reasons for being drawn to Herbert

Place. My mother had a flat there when she was young (second floor from the top in one of the five-storey houses near the Warrington Place end) and loved it with a passion that must have entered her DNA, because it transferred itself intact to me.

What had stayed in her mind was not so much the rooms of the flat (although they were fine ones) but what its big Georgian windows looked out on – the most picturesque vistas in Dublin – ones amateur artists never tired of painting. At the back, there was Mount Street Crescent with the Pepper Canister Church sitting in its island, and beyond that, Upper Mount Street on its way to Merrion Square. At the front she looked on out on the canal's prettiest feature – lovely little Huband Bridge.

Not all of her friends were so enthusiastic. Back then, there was as much hatred as there was admiration of Dublin's Georgian terraces and Georgian country houses. They were the occupiers' architecture in many eyes – the physical reminders of a horrific history, which was already being re-written in the textbooks, but was alive and bloody still in passed-down oral narrative. That was before the decades of censorship and the assiduous re-training of the national mind. People still sang rebel songs without a bother. One of her friends – a textile designer who became better known as a white witch – used to shudder when she stood at my mother's draughty back window. 'I just wish it had a better history,' she said, staring down at the Georgian street vista. 'It's such a secret view and so undisturbed – if only it hadn't been built on all that misery – I can never see it without that shadow. Of course, it's not quite as bad as the older terraces,' she added consolingly. 'If you were further in, or on the north side…'

My mother believed her friend actually did see something, but she herself never did. For her and for me, the ghosts that lingered in the area were not those of forgotten foreign oppressors, but of the hard-drinking bohemia who had made those streets their own in the mid-twentieth century. In my mother's girlhood, a story circulated of how Patrick Kavanagh and Ronnie Drew wanted to end a long-standing grudge by getting together over a drink in a Baggot Street pub but failed because one or the other of them had been barred from every establishment on the street.

The writer Elizabeth Bowen had spent part of her dull young life in Herbert Place, in a house not far from the one Martin and I bought, the high dreariness of her family's colonial existence emerging in her writing as a source of comfort rather than of frustration to her. It was a life in which the natives did not impinge. 'They were simply "the others" whose world lay alongside ours but never touched,' she wrote of them. In her day as in ours, Upper Baggot Street was the local shopping street, reached by crossing the canal bridge, but in her time, she was able to describe it as 'classy' – a world of white cotton coats and chalky cleanliness, where 'everyone had not only manners but time.' In my mother's time, Herbert Place was a red-light district at night.

Edward Carson, the arch-enemy of Oscar Wilde and the man who armed Northern Protestants, also lived in Herbert Place – until he could afford to move to Merrion Square.

My mother was married and living in Ranelagh by the time her magical vistas disappeared. Great ugly office blocks were put up at the back of her old building, which blocked the views she had enjoyed of the Pepper Canister Church and Upper Mount Street; later on, yet more crude offices were put up to the front. They were at the other side of the canal so at least Huband Bridge and the canal itself could still be seen from Herbert Place; but if the memory of past perfection didn't exist in the viewer's mind, the viewer's eye could pass on with indifference now.

Our own house, Martin and I had bought at the peak

of the boom, when both property prices and builders' prices were at their highest. Because it had been home to a multitude of in-demand furnished flats since the 1940s (almost every one of our friends knew someone who had lived in a room of it at one time or another) we couldn't avoid doing the usual knocking-down-partitions, repairing-plasterwork, rewiring, plumbing, floor-sanding, new-bathrooms-and-kitchens stuff; but we were hardly short of space. It was a four-storey house with huge rooms, and we really hadn't needed to demolish the sad old two-storey return at the back of it and rebuild the way we did, no expense spared.

We – ok, I – wanted a galleried library, so we built it. The new room was just over 20 feet high and had floor-to-ceiling bookshelves. Two doorways opened into it – the grand one, which led from the first-floor hall to its gallery, and the functional one in the basement, opening from the shiny new kitchen. We made the fireplace opening as large as possible, and the impressive marble surround came from the entrance hall of an ugly old mansion in Cork which was being converted into a budget hotel for walkers. It was a house that had a lot of blood on its hands, and sometimes I blamed that fireplace and its evil history for all our problems.

'Nobody ever has enough space for books,' I said when Martin protested at the expense. 'Anyway, just think of how great it will look at Christmas. Come on, it's bound to add value to the house,' I added hurriedly, before he had a chance to roll his eyes and we'd start to quarrel.

When we were building it, I never stopped thinking of it as a Christmas room – a pagan forest of ivy swags, holly branches, and dangling mistletoe surrounding a monster tree somewhere in the middle. How Martin and I would have managed to bring in and hang those wagon loads of greenery back in the days when both of us worked right up until Christmas Eve, I have no idea; but in 2008, when I visualized the finished house, that was how I saw it. How it looked at other seasons didn't matter so much to me.

Then, of course came The Crash. As things turned out, we never had a Christmas decoration or Christmas meal in that damn house.

For the first year, in 2008, before we completely ran out of money, every inch of it was a building site. For the second Christmas, Reggie was a tiny baby, and I was exhausted both from minding her and from a pregnancy with complications at the end. After that, we were just broke and had no choice but to let one or other set of parents host us.

I finished my glass of Champagne, and noticed that Reggie had left most of her hot chocolate, which was odd; and her long silence, when I thought about it, was even odder. It was rare for Reggie to stop talking, but there had hardly been a word out of her since we sat down. At least, she looked happy enough – just a bit more intense than usual – her attention entirely on one of the giveaway colouring books. Then she surprised me again by suddenly closing the book she was working on, tossing it aside, and starting on another. Curious I picked up the discarded book, flipped through it, and then looked through it again more closely. 'Damn,' I muttered.

'Damn what?' Reggie asked without interest.

'Life,' I said, as it was obvious she wasn't going to pursue the matter. If I felt like explaining – which I didn't – I could have said, 'another problem I don't need,' because that was all I saw in her book.

What Reggie had done with so much unusual concentration was to race through every page from beginning to end, applying sweat and crayons to nothing except the Christmas trees. Everything else – the Santas, the stockings, even the winsome litter of St Bernard puppies with Christmas hats – had been left in black and white.

I thought one of those dark thoughts I didn't allow

myself to think inside the house, and looked back at the
piles of unaffordable Christmas trees we had walked past.
They seemed to have affected Reggie a bit more than I
would have liked. Even in my own cynical brain, their
pungent, evocative scent was still lingering. For senses as
dulled as ours by the unremitting greyness of daily life,
there had been something explosive about that part of
the outing – as if someone had just detonated Christmas.

I looked at Reggie silently for a while, but there was
no fun to be had today from watching her colouring.
Instead, she was reminding me of a sad Victorian print
I had seen once of London street urchins, stretching
their necks to peep through the holly-trimmed window
of some rich person's house, hungry for any contact at
all with Christmas, no matter if it was indifferent and
second-hand.

I even began to wonder about my own strange wobble
outside the window-blind shop, hoping that it hadn't
been brought on by the same childish forces that were
playing on her. I didn't much like that idea – the notion
that my 35-year-old mind might be so broken that I had
nearly passed out at the sight of a pile of netted conifers.
They were symbolic things, I suppose, but they didn't
symbolize that much to me any more, except the idiocy
that had blown up in our faces: a two-storey galleried
library, indeed!

Sighing, I started doing different arithmetic in my
head. I had heard the price of Christmas trees had gone
up to €60. A friend of mine had put up an early tree for
a party and frightened her straitened guests by telling
them the price of it. I was sorry now I had ordered that
awful Champagne, but even if I hadn't, I still wouldn't
have €60. After I paid our tab, I wouldn't have half of it.

Reggie hardly remembered I was there. In the second
colouring book, she had found a monumental tree, spread
over a double page, and being decorated by a pair of
grandparent rabbits. The grandfather rabbit, in cap and

trousers, was standing on a ladder and was stretching – a bit more than was safe – to put a big star on the top branch. The grandmother rabbit in a dress and apron was holding on worriedly to his legs. 'This one's the best tree,' she said happily when she saw me observing. I smiled back and decided to add to my tab – in the bigger picture, how much could it matter – by ordering a cup of coffee for myself and a chocolate chip cookie for her. They were my excuse to sit a while longer. Like it or not, I had more thinking to do – well, calculating anyway.

On the walk back, I took nearly as much interest in the stalls as Chauncey and Reggie. There was plenty mistletoe this year, but mistletoe I could do without; and holly I could get for free. My mother – thanks to her white-witch friend – had planted a load of holly bushes in the Ranelagh back garden. Most of the berries were intended for the birds, but she always covered one bush with nets so we'd have berried branches in the house for Christmas. I began to think about making a holly wreath for the door – Reggie had seen one being assembled on a children's television programme yesterday and couldn't stop talking about it afterwards. While I was at it, I might even make garlands – the Ranelagh house was awash with ivy, and at least wire was cheap. Just once I could decorate that unlucky library in the style of my back-in-the-day imagination.

I was comfortably lost in this cosy planning when another strange thing happened; no harm was done, but it did make me wonder how fit I was today to be in charge of a child and a dog on a busy street. With all the daydreaming, I had not been watching where I was going, and somehow – to this day, I have no idea how it happened – I walked right into a tree: a huge, standing Christmas tree that came from nowhere. A branch of it almost got my eye, scraping my eyebrow. I looked down in a panic at Reggie, but luckily she hadn't been as dozy as I was and had been able to dodge it.

'Jeez, I'm sorry,' – the voice came from behind the branches. 'We didn't think it was that big. It didn't get you, did it?'

What happened, it seemed, was that two teenage boys had decided to put on display a tall tree, which had just been delivered, but when they cut the net, it had spread more than they expected, blocking the narrow area of unobstructed pavement. One of the boys was now working at clearing a path by tossing to one side some empty fruit crates. The other was struggling with the tree itself, attempting, with some difficulty, to drag it away. As he tussled with the giant conifer its shape became more apparent.

'That's some tree,' I said, unable even to see the full size of it.

'It's the bunny tree,' Reggie informed the street loudly, waving her colouring book.

'Actually, could you just hold it there for a minute?' I asked the two boys. 'I know it's heavy, but…'

'No it's not,' said the voice behind the branches. 'Take your time.'

Reggie was singing now at the top of her voice, nothing too tuneful or coherent, just 'Bunny Tree' being repeated again and again to a vaguely 'Jingle Bells' rhythm.

I knew I ought to quieten her a bit, but I didn't feel able. Something – probably the Champagne was part of it – had happened to my brain. It more or less closed down with the surprise of crashing into the tree. Even when I saw that my silent staring was making the boys uneasy, I still couldn't move or speak. Finally one small part of the brain – the bit that was best exercised in recent times – sprang back to life, and I tried to calculate the amount of money I had in my wallet. It wasn't that much, but I'd be able to pay a deposit and ask for the tree to be kept. I pulled Reggie and Chauncey over to the woman who seemed to be in charge of the stall.

'I'd like to buy that tree,' I told her. 'But I don't think I have enough cash with me. If I gave you a deposit, could you hold it for me until tomorrow – tomorrow afternoon?'

'Well, I don't know, Luv,' the woman said apologetically. 'I'm only minding the stall for my sister for a few days, and I don't know if she'd want me to do that with one of the big trees.'

'I could give you half the price now,' I pleaded, glancing down at Reggie, who had stopped singing as she listened. 'Almost half the price anyway.'

'I'd like to do it, Luv, I just don't know what my sister would say. Them big trees always go as soon as they come in. It's hotels that want them – the same hotels every year, she says. This big fella here came off the truck only a few minutes ago.'

'It's just – I can't get the money today, but…'

'You know the cost of it don't you – a hundred and ten euro?'

'A hundred and ten,' I said flabbergasted. 'I thought trees cost sixty euro.'

'That's the regular trees. These big lads – nobody buys them but a few hotels.'

The same feeling of unsteadiness came over me that had almost knocked me off my feet earlier. I looked around in a panic for something to lean on, but there was nothing near.

'Are you all right, Luv?' the woman asked worriedly. She lifted a box of oranges off a chair that was beside the stall. 'Listen, sit down there a minute.'

'I'm sorry. I must be getting a bug or something.'

'Here, Jimmy, hold on to that child and the dog for a minute, will you,' the woman said to one of the boys who had been moving the tree. 'And give the little girl a banana. Give the dog one too if he wants it – one of them loose ones.' She lowered her voice a bit. 'Are you expecting, Luv?'

I shook my head. 'No it must be…a flu maybe…'

She hesitated a moment. 'Look, I'll hold on to the tree for you if you're sure you want it. I'll tell my sister… well, I don't know what I'll tell her, but I'll think of something. But why do you want such a dear one? I can give you a nice one there for sixty – or even fifty maybe. You must have an awful tall room if you can even fit this one.'

'I have the tallest bloody room you've ever seen,' I said fiercely. 'Twenty bloody feet high. We built the damn thing for a Christmas tree, but we've never had one and we'll be thrown out before next Christmas. This year's our last chance.'

The woman looked at me uncomfortably, and was silent for a while. 'Can you come back first thing in the morning?' she said at last.

The feeling of faintness crept over me again. 'First thing? I don't think I can. Not first thing. I'll need to get the money from somewhere. It might take me a few hours.'

She was looking at me with increasing interest. 'And look at you,' she said kindly. 'The way you're dressed and all. I'd never have thought…but it's the same with everyone now. The class of people who go to the Carmelites now for the Penny Dinners…' She broke off, embarrassed. 'Not of course I meant that you…'

'Not yet,' I said, and started to laugh, and then had trouble stopping. 'But it may be coming to that soon.'

'I hope it's not a moneylender you're thinking of going to in the morning, Luv.'

'No. I'll just sell something.'

'Oh, that's all right. When you've something to sell, you're not getting in over your head. Is it a pawnbroker you use or one of them new places? The pawnbrokers are better.'

'God, I never thought of a pawnbroker. Are there still pawnbrokers in Dublin?'

'One or two.'

I thought for a moment. 'Do you know how they work? In movies, they hold a thing until you've a chance to come back with the money. Is that what...?'

'I think what they do is hold it for a few months, and if you pay them a bit extra, they'll hold it another few months. But if it wasn't to a pawnbroker, where were you thinking of selling things? Online, is it?'

'No. There's a place that buys clothes and things. Designer stuff, they say, but they...'

'Expensive clothes,' she said nodding. 'Are you going to sell that coat?' she asked, reaching out to touch the sleeve. 'It's a nice one.'

It was a nice one – a stylishly cut and extremely warm sheepskin I had bought back-in-the-day for a Christmas trip Martin and I had taken to Vienna.

'No, not this one. I wouldn't survive without it these days. I wear it around the house to keep me warm.'

'Well, my name's Geraldine, if you don't see me when you come back tomorrow, ask anyone and they'll find me.'

Geraldine sent me home with a bunch of bananas for Reggie, with the name and address of a pawnbroker she thought was still in business, and with the promise that her sons would deliver the tree and set it up for me when I came back with the rest of the money. She would also loan me a stand. 'You'll need a big one for that tree. My sister got a deal on some big, heavy lads, but she's never been able to sell them.'

I walked home, feeling happier than I had in years. I would pawn my engagement ring and all my gold jewellery. Gold didn't suit me anyway, and I had stopped wearing the ring. The stone was big, and was almost a bit dangerous when I was playing with Reggie and Chauncey. I wasn't sure how Martin would take it all, but I'd deal with him some way or other. I had Reggie to think about. 'Don't say a word about the tree to Daddy,'

I told her repeatedly on the way back. 'It's to be a big surprise.'

At least, he would be at work tomorrow. He did some part-time lecturing at one of the Institutes of Technology, and he was usually gone all day Wednesday. I would ask Helen and Mary, who lived three houses down, to mind Reggie and Chauncey for me while I went to the pawnbroker. They had offered to baby-sit any time I had a problem, so I didn't mind asking.

Mary and Helen were mother and daughter. Mary was ninety-five, and had lived in that house – in the first-floor flat – since the 1940s, and Helen had been born there. They were sitting tenants – almost the last of their kind on the street now. Even as late as my mother's time, Herbert Place still had been choc-a-bloc with sitting tenants, but most of them had to leave in the 1980s when a change in law allowed landlords to put them out. Luckily for Mary and Helen, their landlord was some sort of relative, so they had been left undisturbed even though the rest of the building now was let to offices. I used to worry about the two of them, although I never let on. I didn't think their landlord-relative would put them out of the flat while Mary was alive, but after she died... Evictions of every kind were so much the norm now – fashionable, even, in the era of banker-rule that had followed the crash.

They were interesting women, Mary and Helen – both nurses and both now retired; and both of them had been married once. At least, I think Mary had been married. I know Helen had because she told me once that she'd got a divorce in England (before it was allowed in Ireland) after about six months. She and her husband had bought a modern house in Stillorgan, but she'd abandoned it to him. 'I never missed it,' she said. 'It was a horrible house.'

When Helen had to go away a few times – once to a wedding and twice to family funerals – I spent the night in the flat with Mary, which I enjoyed. In these bad-tempered days, Mary was the only person I could talk to without getting testy. Luckily she had suffered no loss of hearing with age, although she had problems with her eyesight and she didn't find walking that easy now. She needed a wheelchair when she went out.

She had a gift – invaluable, even if disconcerting sometimes – for seeing the funny side of anything, including of pure misery; occasionally she was taken over by a laugh she couldn't stop – the Long Laugh, Helen called it. I got a fright the first time I witnessed it. What happened was that I was telling her how the State was paying that €200,000-a-year salary to our atrocious mogul, and how, for lack of any other remedy, I'd tracked down some old books on curses, and was looking for a suitable one to put on him. 'There's nothing else I can do,' I explained. 'I don't want to kill him or anything. But I'd like to find one that would keep him incredibly poor and worried about money all the time, and maybe in jail.'

Mary said nothing to this, and then I got uneasy because she was gazing down at her lap, and the bottom of her face seemed to be crumpling in on itself. 'Are you all right?' I asked worriedly, just as Helen came into the room.

'She's fine,' Helen said. 'But you won't get a word out of her for a few minutes. You must have said something that tickled her. That's her Long Laugh. It goes on for a while.'

I watched, feeling awkward at first, as Mary's face got red and discoloured, and then tears ran down her cheeks. She made a few attempts to speak, but couldn't. By the time she got her voice back – and that took what seemed like an eternity – Helen and I were both laughing as well. I decided to say nothing more about the curses.

Also, I loved their flat. Apart from anything else, it was warm all the time – compared to our house anyway. Its only awkwardness was the location of their kitchen – half a flight down from their other rooms, by public stairs, so Mary couldn't really use it any more; but that didn't seem to bother either of them. They kept a kettle and a small fridge in Mary's bedroom.

The rest of their flat – a sitting room and two bedrooms, one of which had been appropriated from the original double-windowed front drawing room – was similar in layout to most first-floor Dublin Georgian conversions, but its style was very un-Dublin: formal, decidedly faded, and unchanged since 1947.

The grandeur had been a present from a wealthy South African woman – an invalid for whom Mary had worked as a private nurse, just after she came back to Dublin from England. When the woman dismantled her lavish Wicklow house before going back to South Africa, she sent some of the nicest of its fittings in a delivery van to Herbert Place: heavily interlined chintz curtains, a silk Persian rug that used to worry me to walk on, a huge sofa, five elegant table lamps, gentle in style, with gold silk shades, and a tall over-mantle mirror. I used to wonder sometimes if they were the reason the flat was so strangely comforting – not just because they were lovely, but it was almost as if the kindness behind the gifts remained resident in them.

On the way back from Camden Street, we stopped in there for a visit. Helen was in the kitchen making lemon curd and invited Reggie and Chauncey to stay and watch. She said there would be no problem about tomorrow – she could mind them all day if I wanted. I said nothing about the window blind.

Upstairs, I found Mary, sitting as usual on the long couch that faced the big marble fireplace, which was identical to ours, except that Mary's always had a fire lit in it and ours never did. I planted myself beside her on the sofa, as close as possible to the fire, and told her about the Christmas tree and my plans for a pawnbroker.

'Catherine, don't pawn your engagement ring,' Mary

said quickly. 'Other jewellery mightn't matter. But anything Martin gave you, I wouldn't pawn if I were you.'

'That doesn't leave much. I've never bought jewellery for myself. Well, a watch once – the first time I got a real paycheck. It was a Cartier, so that's probably worth something – if I can remember where I put it. I haven't worn it since Chauncey was a pup. He kept trying to chew the blue bit off it.'

'Well, that's a start. But you must have more than that – the way the two of you used to spend money.' She looked into the air for a moment, thinking. 'What about those old coins you showed me once,' she said then. 'Do you still have those?'

I turned to look at her. 'What a smart cookie you are. I'd forgotten all about the coins. They'd sell sort of automatically wouldn't they?'

When I was a child, my granduncle in Australia used to send me a gold half-sovereign every Christmas until he died. I had twelve of them, and had shown them to Mary once, asking her if she remembered when they were in circulation. 'What do you suppose they'd be worth?'

'They'd be worth a Christmas tree anyway, and they wouldn't be of any significance to Martin. And if he thought you'd just lost the watch, I'd let him go on thinking it.'

'Will you come down to see the tree when it's up?' I asked. 'I could help Helen with the wheelchair. And Martin could help too. He's an old stuffed shirt, but useful at things like that.'

'Maybe you should go a bit easy on Martin now,' she said tentatively. 'All those money problems ye have – they might be harder on him than you think.'

'I suppose so,' I said without interest.

'I wouldn't say Martin's as adaptable as you are.'

I laughed, and Mary frowned – a rare expression for her.

'Listen, Catherine, Martin's world has fallen away

from under him. I know yours has too, but you're able for it. You can't hold it against Martin that he wasn't born as adaptable as you are. A lot of honest people aren't too adaptable. I was a bit that way myself once. Before that time I was in London.'

'During the war, you mean?'

She nodded.

'Well, going through a blitz might have changed you, but if you want my opinion, I think it would take more than a blitz to change Martin. Honestly, even if he'd been in Hiroshima...'

'I was in Lambeth Hospital the night it was bombed in 1941.'

I stared at her. 'Were you? Seriously? That was a terrible bombing – I read about it in a novel not long ago. Why did you never tell me before?'

'It's not a thing you like to talk about. There were a load of us nurses from Ireland there that night. Some of the girls were killed.'

'Were you hurt yourself?'

Not hurt exactly. But it was an experience. I was buried for a couple of hours. By the time they dug me out, I'd given myself up for dead. I was hallucinating a bit. You might say it affected my head afterwards, all right, but not in a bad way. It was like the bomb blew out of me the little miss I'd been up to then and put in...oh, I don't know, something different. It blew the ambition out of me anyway. After it happened, I turned down every promotion I was offered. And you know – but keep quiet about this, I've never told anyone – not even Helen – I had two abortions during the war.'

I was surprised, although not as much as I might have been. It was obvious that Mary had a past.

'But how were you able to stand it back in Dublin after the war? I mean it's stuffed-shirt heaven now, but then...'

'It was a dry old place all right – not a bit like down

the country. And the funny thing was, I'd been offered a great job in London – a real high-up one for the age I was. But Mother of God, the rationing they had there. After the bomb, life seemed way too short to put up with that. Every day without butter and sugar and meat and tea back then was a day of life lost as far as I was concerned. At least they had food in Ireland – they had ration books, too, but they didn't mean anything. The English used to come over when they wanted a decent meal. All the rashers and eggs they could only dream of at home.'

'Any more secrets?' I asked fascinated. 'I'm surrounded by such dull people, apart from you.'

'The only reason I'm telling you all this now is because – look, don't get mad at me – it's because I can't help feeling sorry for Martin. He reminds me of me before the bomb hit, and I know you wouldn't know what it's like to be that way, but I do. I had my whole life planned out back then and Martin's the same. All he's worrying about is how to keep that old plan of his on course, even though...'

'At least he doesn't seem to be going mad,' I said dully, 'which is more than I can say about myself. Do you know, I ordered a glass of Champagne when Reggie and I were out today – only don't say anything about this to Reggie because I told her it was soda – even though we would have had our gas cut off last week if Martin's parents hadn't paid the bill. Now I can't think about anything but this crazy tree. When I thought for a minute that I wasn't going to get it, I really wondered if I could carry on living – it just seemed as if there was no point to anything – and that was the second time today I had that feeling.'

'Then buy the old tree, and don't think any more about it. Sure what's a hundred euro...'

'A hundred and ten euro.'

'Well what difference is that going to make with the

mess ye're in. It's a drop in the ocean. And a fine big Christmas tree will keep you...'

'Sane?'

'...occupied. That's all I was going to say. It will be a big job doing up a tree like that. Reggie'll be out of her skin with excitement, and – well, as you say yourself, who knows where you'll be next year. But I don't know why you don't try to bring Martin along with you.'

I sniffed. 'He'll see it soon enough. He'd scupper it if he knew anything about it in advance. I think he has this idea that fun is some kind of sin now just because we owe money. It's like we're supposed to be in mourning because we're broke.'

'I don't know why you don't lie to him a bit more. You could tell him they gave the tree to you for next to nothing because it was too big. Say anything you like. Just don't be trying to torment him.'

I didn't doubt her advice was sound, but I had no hope of following it that night – Martin was too irritating. I had got home first, and was making soup of a sort I had never made before. Recession soup, the recipe called it – a fair enough name. I had actually been saving leftovers and boiled them up for a stock – even old bones from our dinner plates. It was all a bit disgusting, but the early signs were that the soup would have a decent flavour to it.

While it was simmering, Reggie and I practiced an entertainment we wanted to put on for Mary at Christmas. Reggie had been much taken by performances of border collies on television dog shows – the ones where they were up on their hind legs and dancing with their owners. I told her at first that I didn't think that would be good for Chauncey, but then I looked it up, and it seemed it was – the exercise strengthened their back leg muscles and they enjoyed it. But they needed about three months to get their balance. The balance part was still eluding Chauncey, but he was enjoying the practice sessions as much as Reggie and I were. We had tried out a few songs and finally settled on Fred Astaire's 'I Won't Dance' because we thought the lyrics might match Chauncey's performance on the day.

We were in the throes of rehearsal when Martin came in. I had been trying – without much luck – to teach Reggie to quickstep and was using treats to get Chauncey to stand, but the treats had run out, and Chauncey had diverted his attention to tearing up the now-empty bag they had been packaged in. At that point, Reggie and I collapsed on the sofa laughing. Then we became aware of Martin. 'Oh for God's sake,' was all he said, before heading upstairs.

I went upstairs myself a minute later, and located my coins and watch. The following morning, I put them in my bag, left Reggie and Chauncey with Helen and Mary, put on sunglasses, and crossed the Liffey, to the pawnbroker recommended by Geraldine. He offered me €700, which I accepted. I still have no idea if it was a good price or a bad price.

With the roll of cash in my pocket, I went to a shop in the Stephen's Green Centre and bought ten of their longest strings of lights. Reggie and I would shop for baubles at our leisure. Then I headed on to Camden Street.

'Well, look who's here,' Geraldine said heartily as soon as she caught sight of me. 'I was just talking about you. And you're looking a bit better too. Here, put those bags in the van, and sit in there yourself as well. Did it go all right for you?'

'It did,' I told her. 'And I'm really grateful to you for holding the tree.'

She hushed me from saying any more, and told Jimmy to hurry up and get it into the van and get Tony to help him, and be careful with his driving.

The tree had no hope of being got in through the narrow, awkward basement entrance, so the two boys cheerfully hauled it up the flight of stone steps to the hall door and then down the library staircase. They had it up on the stand in a few minutes. Then they turned it for me so that I could see which was the best side, but the truth was, it was almost perfect from every angle. 'It's a mighty tree all right,' Jimmy said admiringly. 'And a mighty room, too,' he added, looking at the gallery and at the bookshelves that ran up to the high ceiling. 'It's like something out of Harry Potter.'

I asked them if they would have a cup of tea or orange juice or something, but they said their Mam would expect them back. As they were going out the door, Jimmy asked me to wait while he got something from the van. When he came back, he hurriedly dropped a large plastic bag inside the door. 'My Mam sent this for the dog. My uncle's a butcher.'

The door was closed behind him before I saw what was inside the bag – four magnificent marrowbones, a pile of chops, and what looked like a couple of shoulders of lamb. Astonished, all I could do at first was look at them. Then I took the bag back to the library and sat down on one of the armchairs that faced the huge fireplace. I felt awful that I hadn't even thanked Jimmy, he'd taken me so much by surprise.

For a while, I stared at the butcher's bag as if hypnotized by it, and then, for no reason I could understand, I started to cry. And it was no ordinary crying. For the first time, I understood what the expression 'racked with sobs' meant. My body rather than my brain seemed to be in charge of the crying. It was heaving, creating strange – extraordinarily loud – noises, and I had no hope of stopping it. My big worry was that I could be heard out on the pavement.

Any time before in my life, when I had cried, even because of genuine emotional misery, I had done so quietly. My face always looked awful afterwards, but I had never made any special noise. What was happening now was a new physical experience – and that damn bag of bones was responsible. It was such an elegant little act of decency. Every time I thought about it, something would come over me and I would get even louder.

I ignored the doorbell when it rang. At first, the ringing was normal, but then it became constant, like someone was leaning on the bell. I'd heard burglars did that to check if there was anyone inside a house – well, better a burglar than a do-gooder neighbour, I was thinking to myself, although it would be a pretty deaf burglar who couldn't hear me.

A few minutes after the ringing stopped, I heard the door open, and knew it was Martin. He was calling out my name. A second later, he and Helen came through the kitchen door into the library where I was sitting, both of them ashen-faced. Helen was holding her phone in her hand.

'Good God, what's happened?' Martin asked. 'Why didn't you answer the door? I forgot my keys. I could hear you out the front.'

I said nothing, not knowing what to say, or what my voice would sound like if I spoke.

His eyes were swinging in bewilderment between me and the tree. 'What the… ?'

Helen sprang at him suddenly and silenced him by squeezing his shoulder. He glanced back at her briefly, but would have gone on talking only she grabbed his left ear and pulled it until he looked around again. I watched all this in astonishment and Martin was clearly annoyed, but he didn't say anything.

'She's all right, Mammy,' Helen said into the phone, while still holding tightly on to Martin's ear. 'OK, I'll ask him to go up to you right now.

'Listen, if you're able for it,' she said to me, 'Mammy wants to come to see you, and she's wondering if Martin can give us a hand with the wheelchair. You don't mind, do you Martin?'

Martin – his ear still held by Helen – said stiffly that of course he didn't.

I added – not too coherently – that I'd love to see Mary.

'Go on ahead, will you,' Helen said to Martin, who didn't move. 'Go on, will you, please,' she urged in a beseeching tone. 'I'll come after you in a minute.'

'Well, I'm glad you left a key with us,' she said after Martin reluctantly did as she asked. 'Listen, did something happen to you?'

I shook my head. 'Nothing happened. I just took a crazy turn.'

She looked at the tree and I thought for a minute she was going to laugh. 'Well, it happens,' she said then. 'I'd better go apologize to Martin. He must think I went mad, but he'd got such a fright, I could see an ugly fight coming between the two of you. I wanted to run him past Mam before you had chance to say much to one another.'

She looked at the tree again, and this time, she did laugh, but still said nothing about it. 'You should go splash your face with cold water. You have time. We'll be at least a quarter of an hour getting Mam down here.'

In fact, they took twenty minutes, and they arrived noisily. When the door opened, a disoriented Chauncey was the first in, bulleting through the kitchen to the library, sniffing in all directions. He glanced briefly at the tree but made a beeline for the marrowbones. I grabbed the plastic bag just before he reached it.

The humans followed at a more sedate pace. Martin was pushing Mary in the wheelchair and Reggie was hanging on tightly to the arm of the chair with one hand, and to Helen's hand with the other. None of them had eyes for anything but the tree when they came through the door from the kitchen, but no one said anything. I felt sorry for Reggie, and I even felt sorry for Martin. Mary and Helen had probably given them some bit of information, but both of them had an expression almost of pain from holding in the questions the two women had forbidden them to ask. How they had silenced Reggie on the subject, I couldn't even imagine.

'It's like a tree from a movie, isn't it?' said Mary.

Chauncey was jumping on me to try get to the bag of bones, so I handed it to Martin, who looked bewildered, but said nothing. 'It's a present for Chauncey,' I said. 'Can you mind it for the moment?'

'Can we dance now, Mummy?' Reggie asked abruptly. 'Mary's here, and you said we were learning the dance for her. We can show her now.' Without waiting for an answer, she turned on the Fred Astaire song.

'Oh Sweetie, Chauncey's not ready yet. He's not...he's hopeless. Mary will just be disappointed if we let her see before he can put on a real show.'

'If you're going to show me Chauncey dancing, believe me, I'm not going to be disappointed,' said Mary. 'Come on, you can't let something as tantalizing as that slip out and then not follow through.'

Reggie obliged instantly, not bothering even to take off her coat before launching into her untamed quickstep – a personal interpretation that owed no debt to the ballroom. Her footwork and timing got even wilder when I reluctantly stood up and joined her. She had forgotten everything I'd taught her, but no one could say she wasn't putting her heart and soul into the performance.

Chauncey, on the other hand – distracted by tree, bones and guests – made no effort at all. The wretch didn't stand on his hind legs even once, and didn't even stand on his four legs most of the time. Generally, he just sat there and looked at the two of us.

Still, the show wasn't a total loss – when it finished, no one could stop laughing. Even I couldn't. Martin was laughing as hard as Mary.

After a minute or so, he stood up suddenly and held

the bag of marrowbones in the air. 'Would you dance for the right price?' he asked Chauncey.

Reggie squealed and immediately restarted the music. I was barely able to take off her coat and hat before she grabbed my skirt with one hand and Martin's free hand with the other, and resumed her quickstep, which was even wilder now that she was less encumbered.

This time, however, it was Chauncey who stole the show. With a plastic bag of motivation floating over his head, he was a different dog. To everyone's surprise, it turned out he *could* stand on his hind legs, although he didn't stay there for long and he didn't do much when he got there. Mostly, he just balanced himself, although twice he took a few steps.

Martin himself put a surprising amount of effort into his footwork, although he had never been much of a dancer. He wasn't helped on this occasion by having to hold a bag of meat in the air with one hand and a wildly hopping Reggie with the other. Still – to judge by the level of applause from Mary and Helen – our audience thought we were fine.

Reggie wanted to do it all again, and as an alternative, wanted to give Chauncey a bone.

'Maybe you should give it a quick boil first, Martin,' Mary suggested. 'I don't care what they say about raw food being good for dogs, with the child and all…'

'And I'll put on tea, Catherine,' Helen offered. 'I don't think there's anyone here who couldn't do with a cup.'

Reggie bolted ahead of her to the kitchen. Martin, however, would have stayed in the room only Helen went over to link her arm with his. 'You'll have to show me where the tea is,' she said.

'If I'd known it would be this much fun here, I'd have come to visit a lot sooner,' Mary said.

I giggled. 'What did you tell Martin about the Christmas tree?'

'Nothing, except that he shouldn't say anything to you about it. And he didn't. You have to give him that.'

'How you kept Reggie from talking about it I can't even...'

'You gave Martin a terrible fright,' Mary said suddenly, her voice barely audible.

'I feel an idiot about it all,' I admitted, but changed the subject quickly. 'At least I know Chauncey should be able to put on a show at Christmas. Now that I know he's been holding out on me...'

'You'll be having Christmas dinner here this year, I suppose?'

'I doubt it. Martin and I would probably kill one another if we did.'

'That's no way to be,' Mary said seriously. 'Ye're both decent people, and ye have enough problems without fighting with one another.'

I shrugged. 'It's what happens. It's strange how money can conceal so many fault lines.'

'But it *is* only money. That's why it makes no sense. Ye haven't a problem in the world except money, and it's not like ye don't have plenty company in the mess ye're in. Half the country's the same way – people yeer age anyway.'

'And a lot of them aren't surviving it too well, are they? The funny thing is, I actually used to think Martin and I had lot in common. I had no idea we'd be so different when it came to money problems.'

She said nothing to this, but looked down at her lap, while her face went a bit odd, the bottom of it seeming to fold in on itself. In the past, she had frightened me when she went like that, but now, of course, I could recognize what was happening – she was starting another of those Long Laughs.

I felt a bit annoyed at first as it followed its usual dramatic course – her face reddened, tears flowed down her cheeks, and when she tried to speak, the words were incomprehensible. Hearing it, Helen, Martin, and Reggie appeared for a moment from the kitchen, but Helen determinedly pulled them back again. She couldn't pull back Chauncey though, who came in and sat beside me, fixing a suspicious eye on Mary.

'Ye're different all right,' Mary said when she could finally get the words out. 'Martin's way of dealing with no money is to work himself half to death and do without. Your way is to buy a tree that's bigger than most people's houses, and dance with the dog.'

She had to struggle to keep her voice under control long enough to finish the last sentence, and then let herself get back to laughing. Eventually – as always happened when she was like this – I started to laugh too.

'So long as you don't put it like that to Martin,' I said after a while.

'I'd never do that. Anyway, I don't think poor Martin has the right of it – I think you do, but I'd never say that to him either. I know if I were the two of you, I'd do that disappearing thing you were telling me about. I'd tell the bank to chase itself for the debt, and I'd get out of this house and out of the country, and start all over. The only worry I'd have would be trying not to get mown down by the stampede of young ones doing the same thing.'

I just looked at her for a while after she came out with this – as surprised as I was grateful. 'Well, that's a bit of a bombshell,' I said finally, 'but honestly, Mary, I've never heard anything before in my life that has meant as much to me as what you've just said. I mean, God knows what we'll actually do in the end, but at least – well, at least I don't feel I'm just going mad when someone like you thinks that my way might make more sense than Martin's way.'

She was trying hard to keep talking seriously, but she was going to start laughing again – I could see that.

Like Chauncey, I couldn't take my eyes off her crumpling lower face.

'Well one thing I know for certain,' she said, just before surrendering to the laughter, 'your way is a hell of a lot more fun.'

...'I've driven up this street a thousand times,' the taxi driver said, 'and I never knew there was a real house in it. I thought it was just offices and those bedsits they don't allow any more where everyone shares a bathroom.'...

II

George Washington's Bed

UPPER PEMBROKE STREET

MAYBE THERE WERE other 70-year-old widows even more resented by their son and daughter-in-law than she was, Mrs Moynihan was thinking as she looked wistfully at the photo of the pretty house overlooking Lake Zurich that she was moving out of, in a hurry, that afternoon. But if so, she didn't envy them.

'You have to do something about her,' Clara said to Roderick. 'She's moving into a five-star hotel, for God's sake. It's your money she's spending. There'll be nothing left.'

Mrs Moynihan had not visited Roderick and Clara in Dublin since her husband Con – Roderick's father – had died two years earlier. God, how she missed Con. In the forty-three years they were married, the only night they had spent apart was when she was in hospital having Roderick. Even then, she had fought against going to the hospital. She had wanted to have the baby born at home in her own bed, but that ignorant lump of an obstetrician had bullied her and she'd given in and had it in hospital. What a mistake that was. Still she'd come on a lot since then. A pompous fool wouldn't be able to get the better of her now, although that didn't stop plenty of them from trying.

Sometimes Mrs Moynihan wondered – seriously wondered – if Roderick was really her son, or could that chaotic hospital have made a mistake. She even had a DNA test done once, without telling Con, and the test said he was their son, but she still wasn't convinced. When you thought about it, the people doing the DNA tests could make a mistake as easily as those hospital people. She understood now where the legend of changelings came from; when two decent people found they had a child they didn't understand and didn't much care for – well it was a mystery, that was all. No wonder the old people used to blame the fairies for doing a swap.

The truth was, Roderick didn't even look like her or Con. He had their blue eyes all right, but that didn't mean much since so did most the country. He didn't have their black hair though. Hers was grey now, of course, but when she and Con were young, both of them had hair as black as obsidian. Roderick had red hair, for heaven's sake. Unusual, of course, the doctors said, but by no means impossible, and they drew her one of those family-tree-type charts and talked about recessive genes.

But Roderick was different in other ways too; he was shorter than his father, and more inclined to stoutness. He was even shorter than she was, which she thought was surprising. The truth was, whatever any DNA test said, she'd never forgive herself for going into that hospital.

She had tried to avoid anything to do with hospitals after. When Con died, he did it where he wanted, in his own bed, in their nice Lake Zurich house she was having to abandon now to a family of rich Russians. The Russians would pay her a big rent, but she didn't care about that. She and Con had loved that house. She had expected she would die in it herself when her own time came, but after Con was gone, the house became trouble.

Not because she couldn't maintain it – true, it was a big sort of house with a big garden around it, but the staff she and Con had put together were as efficient as they were decent, and they had got used to running it without any help from her. Lena came from a farm in Uri and she and her two nieces took care of the house. Mikey took care of the garden and took care of her – well, of her mind anyway. After Con died, he and her twin brother, Paul, in Dublin, were all she had left.

Roderick and Clara didn't go for Mikey. He had come back to Switzerland with her and Con in 1998, and stayed. All three of them had expected it would be for a short visit – a thank-you for help he had given them in Ireland – but she and Con liked having him around. He was in a world of his own for a lot of the time in the beginning, but he was a comfortable, quiet presence. They all understood one another.

They had met in a funny way. It was on the last holiday she and Con had taken in Ireland, and it hadn't been a good one – not a bit like the one they'd had in 1995 during the Hot Summer, when it stayed hot and dry every day for a few months. Everyone who was old enough remembered that summer.

That final holiday there was different. The weather was back to the way it always was, and the change in the country had started. She had never met so much rudeness in the space of a week. The last hotel had been the biggest disappointment. It had been perfect in 1995 – a lovely old place not far from Kenmare that had changed over time no more than it had to. The couple who ran it then, the O'Connors, had inherited it in the 1960s from Mrs O'Connor's parents. They were nice people and hotel-keeping had been a bit of a religion for them, but their children had no interest in the business, so they had put it up for sale when Mrs O'Connor had a stroke. A group of investors bought it and the first cousin of one of them was made the manager – a short-tempered woman with a gift for insult.

'You have as many as everyone has,' she had said when Mrs Moynihan phoned down to ask for more towels. 'If you take them with you, we'll send on the bill.'

'There's no place safe,' Con had grumbled. 'They've brought in some tax-break for moneymen to buy these places and those fellows hire sluts to run them. I'm inclined to give up and go home before things get worse.'

They had planned to spend a month in Ireland – three weeks touring the country, and a week with her brother, Paul, in Dublin, in his house in Upper Pembroke Street – but after only five days, the last of which was spent in that disaster of a hotel, they decided to go home. They didn't even have a chance to see Paul before they went because he was still on holiday in Vietnam. Still, Paul would understand. He had warned them they would find the country changed. Anyway, he liked visiting Switzerland. They would send him a plane ticket and coax him to come over and stay as long as he wanted.

They headed off from the hotel in the hired car without much sleep. Both of them had been sick in the night. It was the meal in the hotel restaurant that caused it, they knew, even though they had left most of it on the plate. Mrs Moynihan could hardly bear to think of how good the meals had been in that hotel the last time – good, plain food that tasted as if it had been cooked by someone's mother. Everyone loved it. But now – all they gave you were those funny little mounds of different ingredients that young male chefs liked to throw together and that always looked to her like they'd been handled too much – and on square plates, too. A bad sign, those square plates, she always thought. In the morning, they ordered coffee in the room but couldn't drink it. It was tepid and bitter and had been sitting around so long that it had a bit of a blue tint to it.

That was why they had the accident, she thought. On top of getting no sleep, they had no caffeine, and they had reached the age when they needed caffeine. After checking out of the hotel (and carrying their own bags down the stairs, although they had reached the age when they needed help with that too) they had decided to head straight for Cork Airport. They were nearly at the Kerry-Cork border when the thing happened.

It seemed as if they both fell asleep – just for an instant – at the same time. What she knew for certain was that she woke up to find the car going off the road and into a bank. Con seemed to have time to get his foot on the brake before they hit. Enough to slow them a bit – they were lucky in that. Also, it was only a bank of earth they hit, which was even luckier. And the car they had hired was a big whale of a Mercedes, the same as they had at home, so it was able to take a knock. Neither of them was hurt, but they were shaken all right.

They didn't know what was going on outside the car, but then all of a sudden, Con's door was pulled open – her door wouldn't budge after the crash – and a man with thick glasses – that was all she noticed first, the strong lenses in his glasses – was asking them if they were all right, and would he call an ambulance. That was Mikey. That was how they met him.

They said no to an ambulance, and what happened in the end was that they spent the night with Mikey, in an old farmhouse just up a lane from where they had the accident. It wasn't Mikey's own house – he was staying there minding a friend's dog while the man was on a visit to relatives in America. They didn't intend staying the night, but Mikey insisted they lie down and he made them a pot of tea – the first good pot of tea they'd had in Ireland. It tasted like tea from her childhood.

'The hotels here can't make tea anymore,' she said contentedly, pouring herself a second cup. 'They use machines that don't boil water. They say that's the problem.'

'Well, the kettle's always on here,' he told them. Later he made them ham sandwiches. He dealt with the car-hire company for them, and in the evening, he drove out, and came back with bacon and eggs for their breakfast. His friend's dog – an ancient collie with arthritis and suspicious eyes who had taken up residence under the car after his owner's departure – had gone with him.

They ended up staying three nights in the house, until

the dog's owner came home. Mikey and the collie collected
the man from Shannon Airport, and Mrs Moynihan had
a plate of sandwiches waiting for them. Mikey's friend
urged them to stay longer.

They hesitated because it seemed he genuinely wanted
them to – he was a widower in his 70s, retired from
farming, and he said it was a real treat to have people to
stay. But the house had only one decent bed (they had
slept in it while they were there, Mikey having moved to a
springy old single bed, which he made usable by bringing
in a door from a shed to put under the mattress); so in
the end, they departed that day for Zurich, and Mikey
travelled with them. They left behind as a thank-you a
big new television, an electric blanket, some bottles of
whiskey, and a giant bag of dried pigs' ears for the collie.
Mikey and Mrs Moynihan had gone into Killarney to buy
them the day before.

The Moynihans never returned to Ireland for pleasure
after that. There were mandatory First Communions and
Confirmations in Dublin they had to attend, but they
always kept the visits down to a day.

Mikey, they thought, liked the house in Zurich even
more than they did – the garden anyway. He was from
a farm near Derry. He was half-owner of the farm, but
the running of it had been taken over by a brother-in-
law he didn't get on with ('politics', was his one-word
explanation), and after his parents died, he had turned
his back on it. He didn't know a lot about garden plants
or flowers in the beginning, but he liked the peace of
gardening and he read books about it.

Of course Mikey was a 'political' – that was the word
he used. Most of his adult life had been spent in jail in
the North of Ireland. He had been released only a short
time before they met him, as part of the 'Peace Process,'
as it was called on the news, although Mikey never called
it anything but 'the sell out.' Years before, he had nearly
died on hunger strike – his parents had taken him off it

after he went unconscious. That was what had happened to his eyes – the hunger strike. He had planned to leave Ireland before he met the Moynihans, but had no idea where he would go. 'I never thought I'd end up in a place as nice as this,' he said one day when the three of them were having a cup of tea in the garden, 'and with nothing to do all day except cut a bit of grass and grow flowers. If it's a dream, don't wake me up.'

No, the maintenance of the Zurich house was never going to be a problem to her. The only problem she had with that house was that, after Con's death, she couldn't keep Roderick and Clara out of it. As soon as Con was gone, they acted as if it were their house. They *believed* it was their house, she suspected, although the irony was that Con never had a legal interest in it. Every bit of property they bought, he put in her name. 'Safer that way,' he said. 'Anyway, I've no interest in property. You're the one with the eye for it.'

He had left her a rich widow. She had no idea how rich, and she didn't really care. Con hadn't cared either. He liked the fun of making money all right, and they led a comfortable life, that was for sure, but Con had spent his last years trying to find safe ways to give away most of it. He died before he made much progress. 'You set up a charity and it turns into a racket,' he said. His efforts panicked Roderick and Clara.

Even before he met Clara, Roderick was tight-fisted – certainly compared to her and Con – but within the bounds of many people's normality. After Clara – well the truth was she hardly knew whether to be happy or sad that Clara and her dour, religious, money-grubbing family provided Roderick with a world in which, for the first time in his life, he fitted – and he was the most interesting person in it.

He had been a remarkably joyless child. Even as a toddler, it had been hard to get him to laugh. She had found this so strange that she had forced herself to ask a doctor about it, although her opinion of doctors was low. The paediatrician was bewildered by her enquiry, maybe even implying that it was inappropriate. 'Every child's personality is different,' was all she had to say. 'Problems arise when parents don't respect that.'

Mrs Moynihan nodded, and complimented the doctor on the view from her office, but what she was thinking, she kept to herself.

After a while though, she began to wonder if maybe she was being hard on Roderick without meaning to be – bombarding him with gaiety, although she could see it made him uncomfortable. His birthday parties, for instance – they were almost a penance for him, even though they had been exceptionally good parties, if she said so herself. She had help with them of course, so she had been spared the hard work and was able to assign herself the jobs for which she was best fitted – choosing the sweets and the cakes and the prizes, and of course, the entertainment. She enjoyed thinking up games. For Roderick's fifth birthday, she laid on a treasure hunt, hiding extravagant small presents all over the garden. His small guests – and their mothers – enjoyed themselves hugely. The children looked adorable, she thought, some of them laughing so hard that they had to stop now and then to catch their breath. Poor little Roddy, however, had abandoned the game after the first of the prizes was found by another child, and he couldn't be coaxed back.

For his sixth birthday, she decided to risk one more party and one more treasure hunt, this time stacking the odds in Roddy's favour. As well as hiding prizes as she had done the year before, she hired an actor to dress as a leprechaun and carry a bucket of gold-covered chocolate coins, with one real gold coin buried among them. He was to hide around the garden and run away when he was seen, but whoever caught him and held him would get the treasure. The actor was instructed to make sure it was Roderick who caught him. The poor actor did his best, but Roderick was the only child who ignored him. The game was starting to look fixed by the time two quick little girls saved the day by catching his legs from behind.

She gave up on parties after that.

Roderick's own children were even worse. Roderick at least had manners, but his children didn't really. She suspected Clara had encouraged them to despise her. Clara had been cautious when Con was alive, but when he was gone, she was real trouble.

In the two years since his death, Clara and Roderick came to her house for every holiday, bringing their thousand – well, seven – unpleasant children with them, and they even deposited the two oldest of them, a boy and a girl, with her for the whole of the last summer. She would have been happier having a plague of rats, but she hadn't said a word of complaint to Roderick and Clara. Instead, as soon as she had the chance – the day after those two lumps (she wouldn't waste space in her brain trying to remember their names) went home – she telephoned the agent who had found tenants for that pretty yellow house down the road. A big Hollywood man – a producer or director or something like that – had bought it the year before, but then got divorced and never spent a night in it, and now rich Russians were renting it from him.

'When will it be available?' was all the agent wanted to know. 'I have a list of Russian businessmen with families who'll pay any rent you want for a house like that.'

She told him he could have it in a month's time. She thought she would need that long to get everything packed and get her furniture into storage. But Mikey could handle all that for her. He would be staying on in the gardener's cottage at the edge of the property, which he loved – she wasn't renting that to the Russians. She had left the cottage to him in her will, along with a bit of the garden and enough money for him to live on, although she hadn't told him. There would be trouble about that from Roderick and Clara, she expected, but her Swiss lawyer had been reassuring – even indignant that she would think it possible he might let a foreign lawyer get the better of his arrangements. Lena and her nieces would be going back to their home place, but she would keep all of them on salary. She might find another nice little house somewhere – maybe one she'd say nothing about to Roderick and Clara.

Her plan was to get out of the Zurich house herself that afternoon (just in case the Dublin crowd had any thought of landing someone else on her). She would stay in the *Baur au Lac* for a while. She sent Roderick and Clara an email telling them about the move. If they wanted to join her in the hotel, they could pay for a room. She didn't think they would.

She wasn't going to pack much. She would throw a few things in a bag quickly, and put on that nice new Armani outfit that made her look almost willowy again; but after she got back to her bedroom, she was overcome suddenly by a strange sense of exhaustion and had to lie down on the bed. After a few minutes, Mikey knocked and came in with three cases – a big one, a small one, and a very small one.

'I've never seen you travel lightly yet,' he said, 'so I brought a selection. Do you want me to bring up any more?'

When she didn't answer, he put down the cases and looked at her uneasily. 'You know, you don't have to leave here,' he told her. 'That estate agent won't hold someone like you to a deal if you've changed your mind.'

She had a sudden urge to cry when he said this, but she was able to control herself. 'No, I have to go. There's going to be nothing but trouble if I stay. But how in heaven's name did it come to this? Even if it was in my DNA that I'd fail as a mother, how did I manage to do it with such high drama?'

'You didn't fail as a mother. Your son married a savage

about money. There's plenty of them about, but she's more deceptive than some of them.'

'Except Roderick and Clara don't need money. Do you know what partners in the big law firms make in Dublin? That's what makes it so...unnatural. If they did have money troubles, I'd be glad to help them out but...'

'Believe me, the wife is the real problem. Have you ever seen her pay for something? The money sticks to her hand. It's like a muscle spasm.'

Mrs Moynihan laughed. In fact, she had seen Clara pay a taxi driver once – just once – and that time only because Mrs Moyihan had forgotten her wallet. Mikey was not exaggerating. She had to watch as Clara fished coins with difficulty from whatever fastnesses lurked in the bottom of her bag. In the end the driver had allowed himself to be left short.

'They're a bad lot, that woman and her family. Listen, I'll bring up a couple of more bags and you can fill them all if it makes it easier.'

The phone beside the bed rang, and Mrs Moynihan picked it up.

She said 'Moynihan,' then 'Yes, this is Alma Moynihan.' Then she was silent.

Mikey's hand was on the doorknob, but when he saw her face go strange, he stayed in the room. There was bad news at the other end of the phone line – he could see that.

'What hospital?' she asked finally, in a voice that matched the look in her eyes. 'Can you put him on to me for a minute?'

Mikey went back and sat down at the foot of the bed.

'I'll be there this evening at the latest,' she said. 'Will you be all right till then?' She listened briefly, and then said, 'Put the taxi driver back on to me, will you Paul?' She gestured to Mikey that she wanted something to write with, and he pulled a pen and a notebook from his pocket and handed it to her. 'I can't thank you enough for helping him,' she said warmly, 'but is there any chance you could stay with him for the rest of the day – just until I get there? I'll pay you, of course. – would a thousand euro be all right?' She smiled into the phone. 'That's such a relief – thank you very, very much. Do you have a phone, or should I just ring you on Paul's? Oh, and your name,' she added as an afterthought. 'I know you told me, but…' She wrote down the name Eamon.

She was out of the bed and on her feet before she hung up the phone. 'That was my brother,' she said, on her way to the large dressing room which led off the bedroom. 'He's in an emergency room in Dublin. He collapsed in the street. He was unconscious for a while,' she added in an unsteady voice, 'and the taxi driver brought him to the hospital. He sounded a decent man, the taxi driver, I mean. Paul sounded…'

'I'll book us on a flight,' Mikey said, looking at his watch. 'We're in luck it's Saturday. There's a direct one this afternoon.'

'I'll need cash, but I suppose we can get that at the airport. But you don't have to come, Mikey. I know you never intended to go back to Ireland.'

He laughed. 'Ah well…it might be interesting. Anyway, I'd never let you go alone.'

They arrived in Dublin just after four. When Mrs Moynihan phoned Paul from the airport, the taxi driver answered his phone. 'We'll both be glad to see you,' he said. 'You wouldn't believe this place.' In the background, Mrs Moynihan heard screaming.

'That's not Paul, is it?'

'No, that's a druggie. There's a few of them here left over from last night.'

'God, that's… But tell me what have the doctors said?'

'Jaysus Missus, he hasn't been near a doctor yet. He's fed up waiting. He wants to go home, and he's right, if you ask me, but I didn't think I should take him away before you got here. I was able to pinch a wheelchair – it's only got three wheels, but in this place it's worth more than a Lamborghini. I'll have him waiting for you at the main entrance.' As Mrs Moynihan was thanking him, she heard another loud scream and a crash. She hadn't blessed herself in public for years, but she did then.

She thought the taxi ride would never end, but at least they had no trouble finding Paul when they reached the hospital. As promised, he was waiting for them just behind the entrance doors, sitting in a wheelchair and talking to a man with broad shoulders and a large belly and wearing a short leather jacket. She had no doubt that was Eamon. Paul, she was glad to see, was wearing the good cashmere pullover she had given him for Christmas, which would keep him warm anyway. He had a long scarf draped around his neck, too, which was all to the good. It was only September, but there was a nasty nip in the air – it had felt like January when they were waiting for a taxi outside the airport. His scarf fell with a bit of style, of course, as Paul's scarves always did. She had been trained, when she was a model, to do this and that and the other thing with scarves, but no matter what she did, hers never turned out as good as his. Even looking as sick as he did now – and Mother of God, he did look sick – he had those eyes that people got when... God, no point thinking that way. Anyway she had seen some people who had those same eyes get better when they had treatment – a liver transplant maybe, or even a good course of antibiotics... Well, even looking as sick as that, he was still the most graceful person she had seen all day. It was a strange, frivolous thing to be thinking about in the circumstances, but you couldn't help thinking it when you looked at Paul. Nobody ever could. It was a reason he had always looked so out of place in anorak-loving Ireland, and never more so than now, against the unforgiving fluorescence of the hospital.

'God, I'm glad to see you,' he said in greeting.

As she hugged him, she asked cautiously if he was sure

he didn't want to wait until he had seen a doctor. She and Mikey would wait with him.

'The surest I've been of anything in my life. I'd be waiting a week. Anyway, I don't want to see one. I can't even figure why I let myself be brought here, to be honest. I'd have been gone hours ago, only Eamon said he'd promised you he wouldn't take me away until you arrived.'

Mikey took the taxi driver aside to pay him, handing him the envelope on which 'Eamon, Thank You' had been written by Mrs Moynihan.

'She's wondering if you could hang on for a while when we get Paul back to the house,' he said quietly. 'In case we need help. She'll pay you extra – are you all right with that?'

'All right? Are you joking me? I'll stay a month if you want. It's not like I've ever been paid this much before in my life. Anyway Paul's a decent sort of guy. I'd have worried about leaving him, even without the money.' He lowered his voice. 'Jaysus, they're a dressy pair, aren't they? They stand out a mile in this place.'

He went off whistling to collect his taxi, and while they waited, Mrs Moynihan stood behind Paul's wheelchair, squeezing his shoulders and occasionally rubbing his hair as if he were a child. It was whiter than she remembered, but as thick as it ever was.

Mikey tried not to look at them, but as the taxi driver had observed, it was hard to look at anything else. Everyone who passed by stared at them. For a pair of 70-year-olds, they were remarkably eye-catching – both tall and slim, and the brother obviously was as obsessed with clothes as she was. Mrs Moynihan told him once that, although she had been the fashion model, Paul was the one everyone looked at when the two of them were together. It was something to do with the way he held himself.

'He doesn't really sit, does he?' her boss at the Paris

couturier house had said to her all those years ago. 'He drapes himself.'

She had repeated this to Mikey the first time he met Paul, and he had laughed then at the astuteness of the comment; Paul was undoubtedly a rare bird but he would have been hard put himself to explain what it was that made him stand out as much as he did. Mikey was thinking of the couturier's words now, as he looked at Paul, sick and exhausted and supported only by a stained and unsteady wheelchair, but somehow making the old wheelchair look glamorous.

He was wondering if he'd have a chance to ask the taxi driver privately if he knew what was wrong with Paul when the three of them were startled by a cheery voice calling out: 'Mrs M – I spotted you the second the lift doors opened. You sure haven't lost it – you look like you just walked off a fashion catwalk. Is everything ok? And Paul,' the voice added, 'I didn't recognize you. Hey, what's happened?'

The brother and sister exchanged a look of such panic that Mikey, just noticing it, was inclined to panic too. From some depth, however, Mrs M produced what she called her public smile, and Paul, he noticed with interest, had produced one that was almost identical.

The voice belonged to Eddie Rogers. Both Paul and Mrs Moynihan recognized it. He had been at the same English Jesuit boarding school as Roderick back...oh all those years ago. He used to stay with Roderick sometimes over the holidays, when Paul, too, had been a frequent visitor. He was one of the few friends of Roderick's that she liked and, in normal circumstances, enjoyed running into, but not now. She didn't want Roderick and Clara to know anything about Paul until she knew more herself, but Eddie would tell Roderick – that was certain. That was Dublin for you. It was impossible to pass through it privately. Someone you knew would always pop up where you didn't expect. Eddie was a surgeon of some sort, and maybe this was his hospital, but usually those fellows didn't like doing much at the weekends. She had been unlucky, but that was the way Dublin always worked.

She tried to look happy to see him and enquired about his children. Like Roderick, he had too many of them for her to remember how many – why was it that younger people now, if they had any money at all, seemed to be competing with one another for who could have the most children? Women of her age planned on two, if they could keep it to that. She had found herself that one was enough. Eddie couldn't take his eyes off Paul and obviously wanted to know more, but at the back of it all, Eddie was a kind boy, and when it became evident that Paul didn't want to talk, he kept his questions to himself.

As she chatted, she was wondering would Paul be able to get up from the unsteady wheelchair by himself. If he couldn't, she knew Eddie would insist on helping him, and things might get awkward then; but when the taxi pulled up, Paul made what she guessed was a near-superhuman effort and rose to his feet unaided. As he said good-bye to Eddie, Mikey was already moving him quickly towards the car.

'Well, I won't keep you,' Eddie said politely to Mrs Moynihan. 'But if you need any help, you have my number. Any time, day or night.'

Eddie had a good heart, Mrs Moynihan conceded to herself, but so little discretion that, when they reached Pembroke Street, she was grateful not to find Roderick there ahead of them.

It was evident the day was taking its toll on Paul, although he made a good effort not to let on, and was laughing with the two men as they helped him out of the taxi. Both Mikey and the driver found him a heavier weight than when they had put him in. Mrs Moynihan hurried ahead to open the two locks on the hall door and to undo the alarm. 'His bedroom is two floors up,' she

said, and started up the stairs ahead of them in case the
bed needed to be got ready.

At the landing, she glanced back to see how they were
getting on and then, in spite of the growing lump of fear
inside her, she laughed. It was the expression of Mikey
and the taxi driver as they studied the tall narrow staircase
ahead of them that made her do it. She was reminded
for a moment of a cartoon she'd taken Roderick to see
when he was small – *Cinderella,* she thought it was. She
had a memory of a tired, fat little mouse having a similar
look in its eyes as it gazed up an endless flight of steps
leading to some remote tower. It was the first time she
had laughed since she'd got that phone call. She was
wondering if there was anything useful she could do to
help when Paul spoke up.

'No, the bedroom's too far. This floor is better. In here,'
he said, turning towards the door beside them.

'Are you sure?' his sister asked. 'The bedroom may be a
long way up, but when you get there, you'd be a lot more
comfortable.'

'I'd get stuck there,' he said. 'I'm safer staying in the
library.'

The library was the room off the hall at the front of
the house. It was a smaller room than Mikey expected.
He'd lived in a flat in a Georgian house on the other side
of the city when he first came south, but the smallest
room in that house had been more than three times the
size of this one. He had never been warm in that flat,
but this room you could heat. It was the first Georgian
room he had ever seen that you could describe as 'cosy'.
There was a small, dark marble fireplace – a simple one,
with just two circle things for decoration in each corner
– and it looked like Paul used it all the time. There were
big double doors, now closed, connecting it to the dining
room, from which Mrs Moynihan asked Mikey to bring
in a couple of chairs. All the other walls were lined with
books and bookshelves, floor to ceiling, except for the

chimney breast where there was a tall old painting of a waterfall. There wasn't a lot of furniture in the room, just two armchairs that looked comfortable, two tapestry-covered footstools, an old mahogany chest that was used as a coffee table (and also as a fuel box, he later learned), and a regular table on which there were a few big books and a tray with bottles and a couple of cut-glass tumblers. He could see why Paul liked this room. If he were rich and could stand living in Dublin, it would be the kind of place he'd like himself.

'You know I've driven up this street a thousand times,' the taxi driver said, 'and I never knew there was a real house in it. I thought it was just offices and those bedsits they don't allow any more where everyone shares a bathroom. I picked up a fellow once around here who'd been thrown out of one of those places because he'd taken in a dog — a nice poor old dog. I had to keep her for a week until he found a new place he could sneak her into. In Rathmines, I think it was.'

'You don't think it was in this house he'd been living?' Paul asked interested. 'It used to be in that kind of bedsit, until everyone had to move out in a hurry when the place was condemned.'

'Because of the bathrooms?' Eamon asked.

'No. The back wall — an inspector said it was close to collapsing. It looked like it was made of brick, but the structure was timber, and that had rotted away to nothing. The architect they called in was the son of a friend of mine, and he came to tell me about it. I think he was hoping that Alma might buy it and fix it up, and she did. She had the wall rebuilt. The tricky bit was not having the whole thing collapse while the work was being done.'

'Well, it was worth it,' Eamon said, looking around the room. 'Plenty of space here for old books. That's his business, you know,' he said to Mikey. 'Old books.'

'Wasn't it in Pembroke Street they got the Cairo

Gang,' asked Mikey, 'in some other house that was filled to the rafters?"

'It was,' said Paul, 'but down the other end, in Lower Pembroke Street. In number 28. But they knocked that house in the seventies and put up another building.'

'What was the Cairo Gang when it was at home?' asked Eamon.

'A bunch of British spies during the Tan War,' Mikey told him.

'It's true for you about its being a full house,' said Paul. 'There were an awful lot of people packed into it – all of them British officers and their wives. I read an account that said there were either two officers, or an officer and his wife, in every apartment.'

'Number 28,' Eamon repeated, making a note on a bit of paper he pulled from his pocket. 'Tourists might go for that story. This street always takes their fancy. There's a nice turn on it when you're driving from Baggot Street to Leeson Street.'

'It seems to have run to boarding houses back then,' Paul said. 'Sort of upmarket boarding houses. There was a writer, Elizabeth Bowen – she's not read much anymore – she said her parents lived in lodgings in Upper Pembroke Street before they bought a house in Herbert Place.'

'Have you tea in the house?' Mikey asked abruptly, noticing that Paul's face seemed whiter than before. 'Mrs M will be wanting a cup of tea, and I'd say you wouldn't mind one either.'

Paul looked at him gratefully. 'I'd love one, but I don't know if there's milk. I was on my way to the shop to pick up some when I hit the pavement. The kitchen's downstairs. You could look in the fridge to see if there's any drop left.'

'I'll go with you,' Eamon offered, curious to see more of the house.

Mrs Moynihan moved over to her brother then, seating herself on the arm of his chair. 'Tell me the truth, Paul,' she said quietly, as soon as the door had closed behind the two men. 'Just tell me. I can see how sick you are, but tell me what it is. Whatever you say, it can't be worse than I'm imagining.'

'I don't know,' he said. 'It might be. But what you ought to know first is that I don't mind – and that's God's truth – I genuinely don't mind. It took my head bouncing off a pavement to bring me around to not minding, but...'

'Don't be so mysterious Paul, please. Just tell me. I...' She broke off as the door opened and Eamon put his head in.

'I'm off to the shop for milk,' he said. 'Back in a minute.' The door closed again.

'The fall itself wasn't anything,' Paul said in a low voice. 'The worst part of it was the goddamn helpful crowd that was trying to get me to stay there and wait for an ambulance. If Eamon hadn't appeared, I'd probably be stuck in that hospital now. Thanks for paying him, Alma. I'm very grateful.'

'So you were knocked unconscious?'

'I went unconscious on my feet – that's why I fell – but it was an interesting bit of unconsciousness. When I came to, all I was thinking to myself was – well, this is bad luck. I'm still alive. Honestly, Alma, it was like a cartoon light bulb going on. Waking up was something I didn't want. The single good thing about it was that it gave me a chance to tell you.'

'But what's wrong with you?'

'The same thing Dad had.'

'Oh, God.'

'I'm sorry, Alma. I should have let you know, but I didn't have the guts. If it makes you feel any better, I can guarantee you that dying means nothing to me anymore. I'm beyond resigned. I'm in a hurry, to be honest. The thing I don't want is the misery Dad had for those few weeks, and I've made sure I won't have that. You understand, don't you?'

She stared at him, but said nothing for so long that Paul began to regret being so open with her. He had said too much too quickly – he could see that now, but only after it was too late to take any of it back. In the course of a few seconds, he had told her not only that he was dying, but had made it pretty clear that he was going to speed up the process.

Still, it might be worse. He had been close to telling her even more – how it wasn't just death he was thinking about differently now – it was the afterlife. From the moment he had woken up after that fall, he had been thinking of little else. He was inclined, on balance, to take a positive view of it. There was a chance it would be sublime. Who knew? Nobody obviously. Maybe he could even go on living in this room, which he had loved almost as much as he had loved Alma and Joe, except sitting on the shelves would be the *Codex of Leicester* and a first edition of *Ulysses*. Hell, maybe the authors themselves would be here. He imagined for a moment Leonardo and Joyce sitting on either side of his fireplace with glasses of red wine in their hands. Why not? Maybe you got what you imagined. But how could he have expected that poor Alma would suddenly see it that way? He had grown so comfortable himself with the idea that he had taken it for granted she would do the same; their minds had always run that much in lockstep.

Alma, however, was so lost in thought that she was unaware of her own silence. So far as she knew, she might have been saying out loud to Paul exactly what she was thinking – telling him that of course she understood what he wanted to do and why. He wanted to die quickly – what else would he want with that illness. Their father's death hadn't been good. He had hung on a bit longer that he should have for the sake of her and Paul and their mother, and the memory of that would never stop bothering her. But how was Paul going to manage it, and could she go with him? Did he have pills or what, and did he have spare ones? The more she thought about the notion, the more she liked it. He wouldn't have to die alone, and neither would she.

It was all a bit sudden – a light bulb going on, as Paul had put it – but what was wrong with that? She had no second thoughts. As soon as she decided, she felt nothing but relief. To escape – just like that, and with the person she loved most in the world – from a life that was lonely, messy, and that was making her unkind. She had never been deliberately mean or unkind, but now, she seemed to be drifting that way. Her life had been too good, she supposed. Too much luck was dangerous, she'd known that all her life. Fate – a formidable force, fate – always intervened to balance things out.

Paul was her last link back to the shining years, when she was married to a man who was as smart as she was, and who thought she was perfect. Now she was old, Con was gone, her looks were gone, and she was such a failure as a woman that she had to move out of her house and live in a hotel to avoid her only child.

Mikey would miss her, of course, and she worried about that. She felt more affection for Mikey than she had ever felt for poor Roderick. After Con's death, she wouldn't have been able to go on without him. But Mikey would understand better than anyone – he'd already made it clear that he wasn't one who believed in staying alive just for the sake of it.

'Alma, I'm sorry,' Paul was saying. 'I didn't mean to...'

'Do you have pills?' she asked abruptly. 'Is that what you're planning to take?'

'I'm already taking them,' he answered after a moment. 'That's why I fainted yesterday. They affect the heart – maybe for a short period, like yesterday, or for longer, and you're gone – that can come any time. God I'm relieved that you're here and that you know what to expect now.'

'Tell me more about those pills,' she said, and would

have gone on to ask him how many he had, when a ring of the doorbell made both of them jump.

The sound abruptly brought Alma back to the present. Paul was surprised at how frightened she looked. 'It's just Eamon coming back with the milk,' he said quickly. 'And that's Mikey letting him in,' he added, as they heard footsteps running up from the basement. Then they heard the hall door opening and Eamon announcing cheerfully: 'Hey Mick, look who I found on the step. Paul's nephew. He heard his uncle was sick, and here he is.'

'Oh, damn,' said Mrs Moynihan fiercely. 'I knew it.'

Paul grabbed her hand. 'It's all right, Alma. The poor idiot means well. And it sounds like Clara's not with him.'

The taxi driver proudly led Roderick into the room. Paul was making an attempt to get to his feet when Eamon told him not to be an eejit and to stay as he was. Roderick shot an irritated glance at the driver before going over to shake hands with Paul.

'It's good to see you, Roddy,' Paul said. 'What will you have to drink? I'm told Mikey has set aside his principles and learned to mix a mean gin and tonic. Or there's tea coming, if you're in the mood for that.'

Roderick and his mother were hugging one another stiffly. 'It's kind of you to drop by,' she said awkwardly. 'You heard I was here from Eddie, of course. I didn't want to phone you myself until I knew a bit more about how Paul was.'

Mikey came in with a tray holding a teapot and cups. He and Roderick ignored one another, as they always did. Only the taxi driver was cheerfully oblivious both to Roderick's disdain and to the atmosphere in the room. Mrs Moynihan could have kissed him for it. Eamon whistled while he opened the carton of milk and a package of shortbread biscuits he had bought, then poured milk into the jug, while Mikey went down to the kitchen for a plate for the biscuits.

As Mrs Moynihan started to pour, Eamon and Mikey,

both of them eager for tea, had their eyes fixed on the pot; so Roderick was the only one who noticed when Paul suddenly lost consciousness and drooped sideways over the arm of the chair.

'Good God, he's fainted. What's wrong with him?'

Mrs Moynihan put down the teapot quickly, but before she could go over to Paul, he came to. 'Sorry,' he said. 'Did I just...?'

'You need to be in a hospital,' Roderick told him. 'Look, I'll call up Eddie...'

'No, Roderick, he doesn't want that, and no one is going to put pressure on him,' Mrs Moynihan said sharply.

'At least you need to see a doctor. And you need to be in bed.'

'No, Roddy, thanks. I know it seems odd, but I want to stay right here in this chair.'

'If you have a small bed upstairs, we could bring it down and set it up here,' Mikey suggested. 'I'd say you'd be a lot more comfortable.'

'Well, I don't, I'm afraid.' Paul said, and laughed. 'There's no such thing in this house as a small bed. There is one single bed, but even that is about seven feet high and has decaying silk drapes hanging from it.'

'You're joking, aren't you?' the driver said. 'Jaysus, you're not. Can I have a look?'

'Be my guest. It's on the top floor.'

Mikey and Eamon headed off instantly, but as soon as they were gone, Paul was sorry he had said anything about the bed because, when the two men were no longer around to be targets for Roderick's irritation, he and Alma became the focus of it. Alma, worrying that Roderick would keep on disturbing Paul about doctors and hospitals, seated herself again on the side of his chair and put a protective arm around his shoulders. Roderick looked at her coldly.

'How are Clara and the children?' Paul asked.

'They're well. The kids are writing you thank-you

notes,' he added, looking at his mother. 'They enjoyed their holiday with you.'

'It was such a pleasure having them,' Mrs Moynihan said.

'So you're moving into a hotel. And the *Baur au Lac*, at that. That's going to be something.'

'You know how it is,' his mother said awkwardly. 'I thought I'd reached the age when – well, when there were things I didn't want to have to think about any more. Daily arrangements, things like that. You probably don't have to worry about that sort of business, but...' She let her sentence drift away.

'So you're letting the staff go,' he said at last. 'That will be a bit of an economy anyway...'

'Well, they'll be...well...on a sort of retainer...I mean you never know when...'

Paul was as relieved as his sister when the door burst open, and Mikey and the driver came back into the room, both of them laughing. 'You're feckin' right,' the driver said. 'There isn't a normal bed in the house. I've never seen beds like that in my life. But you know what I could do, I could spin back to the house and pick up one of the kid's beds...'

'For heaven's sake, let me see the beds,' Roderick snapped. He took off his jacket, threw it over the back of a chair, and left the room with the look of a childminder whose stores of patience had just been drained.

'Jaysus, yeah,' said the driver, going after him. 'You should have a look if you've never seen them. I don't know how anyone got them up there.'

Mikey, laughing again, followed the two men upstairs, and Paul and Alma pushed closer together, anxious to take up their conversation where they'd left off; but before either of them said a word, Paul was unconscious. He came to after a few seconds. 'God, I did it again, didn't I?' he said.

'But do those pills kill the pain?' she asked.

'I've separate ones for that. None of them are legal, of course, so the less you know about them, the better. They're effective, though, for the moment.'

'How long have you known?' she asked.

'About a month.'

For a while, neither of them said anything. Paul closed his eyes and rested his head against her arm, while Mrs Moynihan looked around the comfortable room with a feeling more of anger than of sadness. 'It's a wasteful business, mortality,' she said. 'Life dupes us into going to so much trouble about things – this house, for instance, you have it so perfect...'

Paul shrugged. 'On the other hand, what else would I have been doing? The only thing that's bothering me now is you, Alma. I'm afraid you'll have trouble with Roderick and Clara after I'm gone. They'll be trying to get their hands on this house for a start – for one of their brood. But I suppose you don't care...'

'Oh, I do...about *this* house. Because it's *yours*. I don't want Clara messing about with anything of yours.'

'People get different – and meaner – after a death,' he said. 'I've been worrying about that. Do you remember how it was after Dad died – nobody was acting like themselves? I remember thinking afterwards that the world's molecules must get shaken about when someone dies – there was no other explanation for how changed everyone was all of a sudden. And no one changed for the better. You and Mum started fighting and neither of you knew why. And at the same time, I told Mum about Joe and me, which was a rotten thing to do when she'd just lost her husband, but I couldn't stop myself.'

'Listen, Paul, there's no need to worry about me,' Mrs Moynihan began. She was about to tell him the plan she had in mind, but had to break off when Mikey came into the room, bringing pillows and news.

'Hey Paul, you know what you have up there,' he

announced, 'George Washington's bed, and Roderick, believe it or not, figures he can bring it down here.'

'Mikey, were the two of you pulling his leg?' Mrs Moynihan asked. 'He's not really fair game, you know.'

'We didn't say a thing. He got excited, believe it or not, when he saw the damn thing. It's the first time I've ever seen the guy excited. He says he can take it apart so we can bring it down the stairs and put it together again down here, but he was wondering if you had any tools.'

'I do, as a matter of fact. There's a toolbox in the cupboard in the basement under the stairs. You could take it up to him.'

Mikey headed off happily, but came back a few seconds later, helping Roderick and the driver carry a deep mattress they had brought down from the top floor and appeared to be struggling with. 'Feathers,' the driver explained to Mrs Moynihan. 'This is one heavy mattress.'

'Can you really dismantle that bed?' Paul asked. 'I could never manage it. The dealers who brought it in were specialists, but they're based in England.'

'It's easy. I spent a summer taking apart beds like that.'

'Roderick, you didn't,' Mrs Moynihan said indignantly. 'When did you spend a summer doing anything of that sort?'

'In America, the summer I had the student visa working there.'

'But you worked in a bar.'

'No I didn't. I started with a bar job, but it didn't work out. I hadn't the personality for it, the owner told me. But he had a brother who was an antique dealer in New England, and he arranged for the brother to give me a job. Mainly I was to take apart the furniture – 18th century stuff mostly – that was too far gone to be fixed up but had bits that were re-usable. It was up to me to separate those out. It was a great job, to be honest – a lot more interesting than the bar work. We sold George Washington's bed that summer – at least, the customer was told there was a good chance it was George Washington's bed. But not by me,' he added quickly. 'I said nothing.'

'Is that legal?' Paul asked laughing.

Roderick shrugged. '*Caveat emptor*, I suppose. I'd say in that line, pretty much anything goes. I can't imagine the customer believed it really was George Washington's bed, but who knows? It would have given him something to tell his guests anyway. In fact, it was made from a bunch of different beds. Some parts, like the pegs, were newly made, but even that wasn't a total cheat, because they were carved out of 18th century wood. Then we dirtied them up a bit, so you really couldn't tell. It was fun, to be honest. Your bed, Paul, if you're interested, has three new pegs and one old one. They all seem to be ok.'

'Roderick, why did you never tell me that before?' Mrs Moynihan asked. 'I always thought you were just working in a bar in New York.'

Roderick didn't answer, and Paul filled in the silence. 'Did you put them together as well as taking them apart?'

'By the end of the summer, I was the main re-assembler.' Hearing the pride in his voice, his mother felt a strange sense of sadness. 'I assembled about ninety percent of George Washington's bed.'

'Well, hurry up and bring the bits down,' Paul said enthusiastically. 'Before I conk out again. I have to see this.'

'Do you think he was telling the truth?' Alma asked, when she and Paul were alone in the room again.

'Of course he was. Roderick isn't capable of lying. It's one of his problems. And honestly Alma you should be ashamed of yourself that you didn't know. He was only a kid, and without enough personality to work in a bar, for God's sake, and you didn't know that he assembled George Washington's bed?'

'Well, I am ashamed,' she said unhappily. 'I just find it hard to believe.'

The bed came down in bits, some of them mysterious,

and, under Roderick's instructions, was put together again. It looked odd without the draperies, but there was a silent consensus that they'd leave the ancient silk upstairs for the time being. Everyone spent a surprising amount of time just looking at it. Mikey and the taxi driver couldn't stop grinning. If Roderick had made a moon rocket out of a washing machine in front of them, Paul was thinking, the sense of appreciative disbelief in the room could hardly have been stronger.

Mikey startled Mrs Moynihan by going over suddenly to shake Roderick's hand – a sight she had never expected to see, and it was obvious that Roderick hadn't either. 'Cometh the moment...,' he said, letting the line drift.

'But is it comfortable?' Mrs Moynihan asked.

The taxi driver immediately stretched out on it. 'It's okay,' he pronounced. He shifted around and then added, 'Damn comfortable, in fact.'

'Do you want us to bring down pyjamas?' Mikey asked. 'We could give you a hand getting into them.'

'Thanks,' Paul said 'I could probably use the help. But maybe not you, Alma,' he said, smiling at her. 'You know how it is.'

Mrs Moynihan kissed him, then she surprised Roderick by kissing him too – she felt like kissing all of them, but she didn't – and went down to the kitchen to see if there was anything there in the way of food. There wasn't really. She would ask Eamon what could be got easily. Eggs, bread, and butter would do. Mikey could scramble eggs for all of them – Lena had taught him to make good scrambled eggs – to stop him from all that frying, as she put it. Alma was thinking about the bonus she would give that invaluable driver before he left. That was something to look forward to. She enjoyed giving money to decent people. For moments like this, she thought, money was something to be respected – a real force of good.

As soon as his sister was out of the room, Paul gestured to the three men to come closer, and he lowered his voice to almost a whisper. 'Look, guys, you've probably guessed already from all this drama that I'm on my way out; and it's all right, Roderick, Alma knows, and she's ok with it. There's something, though, I don't want her to know about.

'There's a package upstairs – on the top shelf of the hot press. It has plastic sheets and other bits and pieces. A friend of mine – my partner actually, Joe – organized it for himself when he was dying. He planned to die at home, and be laid out at home, but his family didn't go for that. They couldn't face – the details of it all, and I'd say Alma couldn't either, if she knew what was involved, so I don't want her to know.

'But this bit's important: I want to stay here – in this room – until I go to the graveyard. Inside the packet, there's a phone number of a nurse who'll be able to do everything that needs to be done. There's even a burner for frankincense and some other stuff for – you know, cleaning the air, I guess. The nurse is the one who advised him to get them – she's done this before.

'I want Alma to be here when I go,' he said to Mikey, 'but I don't want her to know about the mess or bother. I think there's even a nose clamp in the packet, so that gives you an idea. And I want to be buried beside our parents. Joe and I had wanted to be buried together but his family cremated him, so…'

'Understood,' Mikey said.

Roderick hesitated a moment, but finally he nodded.

It took a while before they had the bed prepared and Paul lying in it. He passed out briefly again, but this time, no one paid much attention. Roderick put a chair beside the bed for his mother, and when she came in, she asked Mikey if he would go to the shop. He was out for about half an hour, and then he reappeared with the eggs, bread, and butter she had asked for, and also with a bottle of whiskey, a bottle of brandy, a six-pack of beer, and a bottle of Champagne.

'You didn't have to buy drink,' Paul protested. 'I have a whole cabinet full.'

'That's good, because this little supply won't last long. But I had to get the Champagne for Mrs M. It's the only drink she really goes for. So where do you keep the glasses for it?'

Roderick found and laid out glasses, and Mikey, at Paul's suggestion, lit a fire in the grate. Then he and Eamon went down to the kitchen, Eamon fixing the toast and Mikey preparing the scrambled eggs – cooking them slowly, as Lena had taught him.

They drank while they were eating, and they drank when they had finished eating – even Paul who sipped Champagne from a tumbler, and directed Mikey where to find a half-dozen more bottles of it down in the basement. The alcohol affected them all less than it usually would. None of them got drunk, although Paul dropped in and out of consciousness – the first time, with a glass in his hand.

He died – surprising everyone – at about four in the morning. Roderick wanted to call the doctor immediately, but his mother shook her head.

'Yes, all right, I know he wanted to stay here,' Roderick said worriedly. 'But we need to call his doctor anyway. He'll know what to do. When you were out of the room earlier, Paul wrote down the name of the one he wanted.'

'Not yet,' Mrs Moynihan said. She had closed Paul's eyes, but had trouble propping his chin up. Finally, with Mikey's help, she wedged it up with pillows, which they covered with a blanket. 'I need to light a candle for him. There are some candle-holders in the dining room. They'll do.'

'Mum, we really need to call the doctor now,' Roderick said again, as Mikey and Eamon went to find the candle-holders. 'We don't want any questions asked about this. We have to avoid a post-mortem. I'm pretty damn sure there are things in his system that shouldn't be, and with all of us here...'

'Not now, Roderick, please. Just help me clear this table and we'll bring it over here beside the bed. I want the candles lighting beside him.'

'Mum...'

Mrs Moynihan suddenly put her hand to her mouth. 'You know, I never asked Paul where he wanted to be buried,' she said unhappily. 'I had the chance. I just never thought.'

'With Gran and Grandad. He told us earlier when you were downstairs. He left very full instructions. In the meantime, he wants to stay here in the house. He also left the name of a woman who could lay him out.'

'Oh, thank heavens for that. I was wondering how we'd be able to arrange everything.'

'But we should call the doctor now. There's a death certificate to...'

'Yes – in a little while. I just want to sit here with him quietly first.'

'I should phone Clara too,' Roderick said uneasily. 'She'll want to know why she wasn't told straightaway.'

'Yes, of course, you must, Roderick, but not just this minute. Talk and explanations take energy that I don't think I have at the moment. I just want to sit with him.'

They phoned the doctor at five and he came before five-thirty. He was a quiet, middle-aged man and seemed to know Paul well.

'Will you be selling the house now?' he asked. 'Paul told me how you bought it for him.'

The question surprised her. 'I don't see how I could. Not with all Paul's things in it. I couldn't bear to disturb them. I might even live here for a while.'

'Would you?' said Roderick. 'What about the *Baur au Lac*?'

She had almost forgotten about the *Baur au Lac*. 'I don't know now. I'm not sure. I was thinking about things earlier when Paul told me he was going to die. I had an idea then I might do something quite different. I suppose I didn't expect he'd die so quickly. I thought I'd have time.'

'Will the funeral Mass be in Westland Row?' Roderick asked his mother. 'That's his parish, isn't it?'

'Oh, I don't know if there will be a funeral Mass. If he didn't say anything about a service, then a burial with Mammy and Daddy was probably all he wanted.'

'But that's...' Roderick began, but stopped when his mother shook her head and looked away. She was trying to think of how she might distract him. She racked her brain for something to do with religion.

'Listen Roderick, even though Paul wasn't practising any more, he always kept the rosary beads Mammy gave him for his Confirmation, and they meant a lot to him. I'm certain they're upstairs – I suspect they're in a drawer in his bedroom. Will you go have a look? I'd like them to be buried with him.'

'Well, of course I will,' said Roderick, pleased by the request. 'I'll find them.'

After he left the room, the taxi driver stood up awkwardly, and Mrs Moynihan went over to him. 'Eamon, it's time you went home. I can't tell you how grateful I am. And Mikey...the other envelope in my handbag... wherever my handbag is. Will you find it and give...will you give it to Eamon. Just give him the entire envelope.'

'Listen, you have to promise to give me a call if you need anything,' Eamon said. 'Any transport or...lifting or anything at all. And it's on the house.'

'He thinks you're a hell of a tipper,' Mikey said when he came back, after seeing the driver to the door. 'Paul was lucky to have landed on him. He made things easier, didn't he. Listen, do you really mean it that you're going to move in here?'

'I don't know. When I was talking to Paul earlier, I thought I'd decided what I was going to do, but then when I saw Roddy putting together that ridiculous bed...'

Mikey laughed. 'He surprised us all with that. I just wish I had it on video. Lena's not going to believe me when I tell her.'

'To think I didn't even know about that summer job of his in America.'

'Nothing strange about that. Students never tell their parents anything.'

'What's wrong with me, Mikey. I did the best I could – I think – but there's just something lacking in me – something other mothers have that makes them accept their children as they are.'

'I don't know what mothers you're talking about – ones in movies maybe. Anyway, most people would swing for Roderick's childhood. You hired a leprechaun for him, for God's sake. Besides, the guy has a life he's happy with now, even if you're not too impressed with it.'

'I suppose so, but...'

'He's a follower, Alma. He's happy having Clara and her family doing his thinking for him. He's not like you and Con. He was bound to end up with a wife cut from a different cloth than the two of you.'

'Well, he found one, that's for sure.'

'She found her rich guy, you mean.'

Mrs Moynihan laughed. 'You don't really think Clara targeted Roderick, do you? Roderick's not the type to be targeted.'

'Come on, Alma, you can't be that innocent? He's rich. What other type gets targeted?'

'Oh, I don't know, Mikey, women...'

'There's not many besides yourself who wouldn't see it. You and Con were an odd pair about money. Both of you found it easy to make, and neither of you put any value on it. Nearly everyone else is the opposite – they don't know how to make it, but they value nothing else.'

'You don't think he was just attracted to her? – she's so much the opposite of me, maybe that appealed to him.'

'God, you're worse than innocent. Of course, he was

targeted. Don't forget their first baby – the fat boy – was born six months after the wedding, and she's not from a family who believes in fooling around outside marriage. You've seen that gilt-edged prayer book of hers. She sits in the front pew at Mass, too – I have that from the Italian lady who helped out the last time the whole bunch of them landed on you. Her theory is that Clara got pregnant, told Roderick that she'd never think about abortion so they'd have to get married. She tells me the gilt-edged-prayer-book set still pull that trick a lot – getting themselves pregnant to force a marriage.'

'Well, maybe she's right. I just find it hard to imagine any woman targeting my poor boring Roderick. People do love money, though, don't they?'

'It's the only thing most of them care about.'

She said nothing for a moment, trying to remember Roderick as he had been before Clara. 'I suppose he would have been a sitting duck,' she said finally. 'Any little bit of flattery and she'd have had him eating out of her hand. He got so little from me, he would have been hungry for it. Do you think Clara's my punishment, Mikey – my punishment for being an awful mother?'

Mikey laughed. 'Well, whatever kind of mother you were, you'd never deserve that cruel a punishment. He was an easy mark, that's all – a not-too-smart only child of extremely rich parents. You couldn't do anything about that. But he's not a bad sort, I was thinking today. He was even kind of likeable upstairs when we were taking apart the bed. He's so susceptible that if he were around decent people more of the time, he'd…'

He broke off as they heard Roderick's footsteps on the stairs. He came into the room triumphantly, with the rosary beads in his hand. 'I found them in the bottom drawer of the tallboy,' he said, pleased. 'There were old photos there too that you should have a look at – interesting ones.'

'Roderick, you prince,' Mrs Moynihan said with a

warmth that took her son by surprise. She stood guiltily to hug him when he brought over the rosary beads, holding him longer and more tightly than she had done since he was a tiny child. Roderick didn't fully return the hug.

'Well, now, I think it's time you told Clara,' she said in as bright a voice as she could find. 'Only you shouldn't tell her on the phone. You should go back home and tell her in person. And you should get a few hours' sleep.'

'I think I should stay until Paul is laid out. Until the woman who's doing it has come and gone.'

'He's right,' Mikey said quickly, remembering the contents of the packet. 'I could light a fire in the room upstairs for the two of you while that's happening. You could lie down on the sofa up there for a while. Paul's not going anywhere.'

At his last words, Mrs Moynihan laughed and Roderick looked irritated. His automatic stiffness exasperated her, as always, but this time, rather than let him see her annoyance she reached out and stroked his hair – a gesture that startled Roderick and even surprised his mother a little. She had been in the habit all her life of ruffling Paul's immaculate hair, just to see it fall back into place perfectly every time. When she did it at the hospital, it had been reassuring to her that he felt so unchanged.

With Roderick, though, it was different – her slight contact with him now brought back no memories at all. She had no perception of anything that felt the same or that seemed different.

Almost experimentally, then, she kissed Roderick on the forehead. Having accomplished this, she did it again. Roderick looked alarmed and Mikey quietly left the room.

Mrs Moynihan was feeling steadily more disturbed by her unfamiliarity with her own son and by Roderick's discomfort with her. But what could she do at this stage of their lives? If only she could pet and kiss Roderick back to infancy, she thought wistfully, so the affection might achieve something. Maybe this time she would succeed in kissing some joy into him, and this time not hold it against him if she failed.

Well, she would pay for her failures now, that was for certain. Her only chance of making amends depended on her going on living – a prospect that had become almost unbearable to her, when all she craved was to stretch out on one of those crazy, huge beds upstairs and die here today in this house with Paul. Of course, she would have to find those pills of his anyway, before anyone else did. Mikey would help her. God, now that she thought about it, wasn't it lucky that Roderick hadn't found them in the tallboy when she'd sent him to look for the rosary beads – she'd taken a risk sending him to poke around like that.

With a growing sense of resignation, she began to suspect that Paul was probably right in his theory about the world's molecules rearranging themselves unrestfully after a death. How else could it have happened that Clara had suddenly become part of her future? How clever, yet wicked, the world was to give her that particular penance.

'I don't think you can have any idea, Darling, how much I appreciate what you did today,' she said, cupping his son's cheeks in her hands while she looked straight into his eyes, an intimacy that she could see he found even more awkward than the kisses. 'There were so few things that could be done for Paul in the end, and you did something that nobody else could, and it made such a difference to him. And to me. I'll never forget how all of us were laughing nearly up to the end. You helped give him the kind of death everyone wants. I'm incredibly grateful to you.'

'Well, we have that anyway,' he said.

...When I was young, my friends used to love visiting Merrion
Square. Sometimes I wished I were less my grandfather's
grandchild, and could see the Square through their eyes.
We all thought the houses were beautiful, but I was never
able to find their history romantic, the way my friends did...

III

Grace Kelly's Dress

MERRION SQUARE

FOR MY FORTIETH BIRTHDAY, Connie and Toby, who lived on the top floor of my house, and Bea and Paul, who lived in the basement, clubbed together and bought me a 1950s cocktail dress from a vintage shop in London. Black on top, it had a flared chiffon skirt that was white except for a branch pattern outlined faintly in black near its undersized waist. Lifting the dress from the tissue paper, I felt the respect of a priest raising a chalice – it was that unnaturally beautiful. It was also strangely familiar. But the waist...

'No, it's okay,' said Bea, seeing where I was looking. 'I measured. But you'll need a corset. We bought one of those as well.'

They had bought the corset from an American online shop. It promised to reduce a waist by up to six inches. 'With this thing, they say it's an advantage if someone has muscles as wasted as yours,' Connie said encouragingly. 'When there's no resistance, it's easier to pull things in. Your muscles are so useless now we should get you down to almost nothing.'

Wasted muscles or not, it took Connie and Bea, working together, half an hour to get me into the thing. It might have taken less time if any of us could stop laughing, but none of us could. Getting the dress itself on was a quicker job, but the fear of doing damage made us cautious. We all worried about putting too much pressure on fragile old seams as the fit was so tight, but in the end,

we had to risk it. 'Praise be to God,' said the religious
Bea, when the sewing held.

I headed straight for the mirror, but found they had
blocked it with a canvas – the still unfinished portrait of
an American hedge-fund manager I had put aside when
my shoulders started acting up.

'Not till we're done,' said Connie. 'You have to see the
whole outfit at once.'

'There's more?'

'This, for a start,' she said proudly, holding up a
vast petticoat of white tulle. 'Paul's aunt made it – his
dressmaker aunt. It's something, isn't it?'

'It came all the way from the Philippines?'

Connie nodded. 'More planning has gone into this
birthday than into D-Day.'

Paul was Bea's husband. The two of them had come to
Ireland from the Philippines ten years earlier when Bea
got a job as a hospital nurse. Paul had worked for a builder
in Manila, but couldn't get a work permit in Ireland, so
spent his days in Dublin attending a few language classes,
but mainly doing repairs on my old house, which was a
never-ending job. He was shyer than Bea, with such a
terror of conversation that Connie and Toby and I had
got used to seeing him scurrying away when we came
near. He was happiest working and could turn a hand
to most trades. Thanks to Paul's relentless attentions, the
house was probably in the best shape it had been in for
more than a century.

On the evidence of the petticoat, Paul's aunt didn't
mind work either. When we had the entirety of it
positioned under the dress – another job that took the
three of us – the floating chiffon might have filled a small
room. It flared even more when I turned around.

'My God,' said Connie, 'you just did a twirl.'

'I had no choice. The dress made me do it. I mean,
look at it.'

'There's more,' Bea said happily, handing me a shoebox tied with a ribbon. 'This is from your mother.'

Inside the box was a pair of black patent-leather pumps nestled in a bed of silk. They were elegant things – simple, shiny and new, with almost pointy toes, and heels that other women might regard a low, but which were high for me – nearly an inch an a half. 'They're beautiful,' I said gazing at them wistfully, 'but...' I looked down at the fluffy red socks which were the footwear I favoured now.

'Oh, do take off those awful socks,' said Connie. 'It's annoying seeing them so close to that dress.'

The shoes were deceptive. They looked like regular pumps, but in fact they were wide – very wide indeed – where I needed width, narrow where I didn't, and there was a mountain of soft support under the toe joints and arches. I found their comfort bewildering. 'Where on earth did she get them?' I asked.

'She had them made from the casts they took of your feet last year when you had the orthotics done,' Bea said. 'You will be able to wear them, won't you?' she asked worriedly. 'I think they cost a fortune.'

'I may never take them off. But I'll have to shoot you both, you know, if you won't let me look at that mirror.'

They pulled aside the obstructing canvas, and what I saw first made me jump – it was like the reflection of two different beings. I took a quick step forward to stop myself seeing anything above the neck. That brief glimpse of my face and hair had threatened to spoil the moment, but as for the rest...

'This is one gorgeous dress,' I said. 'I've never even *seen* one that looks as good. From the neck down, I could be a different person.'

'You look very beautiful,' said Bea. 'You look like a model.'

Sadly, this was a shameless lie. Whenever I saw my face these days, it appeared over a bathrobe or an old shirt, and then it looked bad enough; but rising above this extravagant, perfect dress, it looked close to gruesome. My skin had been normal once, but so long ago that I could hardly remember. Now it was marked by mysterious rashes on the forehead and cheeks, and sagged from a decade of near immobility. Under each eye was a white, puffy mound, and under each of these was 'the blue semicircle of ill health' as Scott Fitzgerald prettily put it, although in my case the colour was more of a blackish purple. More than three inches of grey roots were showing. I had got used to this unholy vision and it hadn't bothered me too much for years, but when I saw it together with that dress...

'It's true,' said Connie. 'Whatever it's done for the arthritis, at least your regime has made you damn thin. That dress looks sensational on you.'

'So long as I can't see my face, I feel like...oh, hold on. I know where I saw this dress before. It was the one Grace Kelly was wearing in *Rear Window* when she brought the waiter from "21" with James Stewart's dinner.'

'We knew you'd remember,' said Bea, giggling. 'You always remember dresses.'

'How on earth...?'

'The shop thinks it was a rip-off that was made after the film came out – in Hong Kong, apparently,' said Connie. 'It's good isn't it?'

'I think it's all hand-sewn,' I said, looking at a seam inside the skirt.

'Go on, twirl again,' said Connie. 'You know you're dying to.'

'You'll need the dress for tonight,' said Bea, as she and Connie stepped back to let the skirt flare out to its fullest. 'We're giving you a party.'

'And you'll need the corset even more,' Connie added. 'Wait till you hear who's doing the cooking.'

'A party?' My voice was sharper than I intended. 'You haven't invited people, have you?'

'Your mother and Jasper are coming,' Bea explained quickly. 'That's all.'

'Which was supposed to be a surprise,' Connie put in, 'but we all knew you'd panic the information out of us.'

'Oh, that's ok,' I said, relieved. 'I mean it's great actually. I thought my mother might be planning something. She had a suspicious sound when she was on the phone. So who's doing the cooking?'

'Toby's boss. Remy Decona. With his own medal-winning hands.'

I looked at Bea to see if Connie was serious. Bea nodded her head.

'He's already started in a kind of a way,' Connie said. 'Paul and Toby brought over two of his bottle-gas cookers last night after you'd gone to bed. Your old electric cooker didn't impress him much – Toby showed him a photo. You don't want to know what he said.'

'But what about his restaurant?'

'*Como* doesn't open on Mondays.'

I wasn't sure which to worry about more now – the state of my face and hair, or the state of the old basement kitchen that I'd always meant to fix up. 'Well, I'm... I can hardly take all this in. How on earth...?'

'He wanted to do something for Toby, and Toby suggested this.'

'But cooking a dinner *here*! – Did Toby bury a body for him or something?'

'Close.' Connie lowered her voice. 'Saved him from the taxmen – he was almost shut down. He owes them a fortune, but he's been offered some television work in England next year and a cookbook to go with it, so Toby was able to convince them that he'd be able to come good in the end.'

'Golly.'

'And there's more. Toby also did something mysterious for Sasha – the Ukrainian headwaiter – when the immigration people had him in their sights. And don't ask me what – I have no idea.'

Toby was Connie's latest, and most interesting, boyfriend. He was from Australia and had been on a quick visit to Dublin when he met Connie and, because of her, decided to stay – working at this and that, including a part-time waiter's job at the suddenly very fashionable *Como* restaurant.

In my eating-out days, *Como* had been a pizzeria used by students and bargain-loving tourists, but it had been taken over and re-named five years ago by Remy Decona – from somewhere in the Balkans, no one was sure exactly where – and since then had transformed itself into the most booked-out restaurant in Dublin. Out of nowhere it had even been awarded a Michelin star. The teeth of other restaurateurs were still grinding.

Connie had been living on the top floor of my house for nearly ten years. My mother had found her for me at a time when I was in a bad way – when I was bed-ridden and had to have both a cook and a nurse in the house. It was rheumatoid arthritis – 'profound rheumatoid arthritis', as the doctors tiredly put it, when none of their drugs did any good – neither the new ones nor the old ones; and even the steroids that made me swell like a dirigible gave only minor relief. My mother stayed with me after I left the hospital and was as panicked as I was. She telephoned clinics all over the world that were supposed to know something about it, and the conversations had left her desolate. 'They're so cold,' she said, 'and belittling. Almost hostile, some of them. And I really don't think they know much about the disease. It's as if they blame you because their wretched medicines have done nothing for you.'

Finally she made contact with a nice woman in California who said that, if it were her daughter, she'd take her to this herbalist in New Mexico she'd heard things about. 'You'll need an open mind,' she said. 'Some of what she does sounds like borderline witchcraft, but I know of two bad cases she seems to have helped.'

My mother flew to New Mexico two days later, and spent a week with the woman – Melissa, by name – who was a quarter Paiute Indian, a quarter Cherokee, a quarter Irish, and a quarter Hungarian, and she came back sparkling.

'You're going to be fine,' she told me as soon as she came through the bedroom door. 'Forget what you've been told – rheumatoid arthritis is perfectly curable.'

Untrue, of course, but Melissa had instructed her to say it with conviction and to make sure I believed her because no other part of the treatment would do as much good. I know for certain this was smart advice, because as soon as my mother said the word 'curable', I could feel – literally feel – something change inside me. It was physical, not just psychological. The cells that made up my body may have been a sorry bunch, but luckily they were gullible.

It was by pure chance that Melissa's daughter was studying in Dublin at the time, doing a PhD in medieval history at Trinity. She was living in Portobello with four other students, in a shared house with failed heating and a mould problem, and jumped at the chance to move to a large flat in Merrion Square, even though 'tending to' me, as her mother put it, was part of the job.

The arrangement between us was expected to be short-term, but suited us both so well – 'the instant compatibility of weirdos,' in Connie's words – that she never left. Connie was sensitive, intuitive, and as discreet as she was trustworthy – qualities rarer than yodelling pandas in gossipy Dublin. After a few months, she abandoned the PhD. 'I'd never have finished it anyway,' she said. 'The research grant seemed better than getting a real job, but God it's a relief just to throw it there. I couldn't imagine years more of that.'

Being her mother's daughter, Connie knew her decoctions from her infusions, and as automatically as

I used to enquire about the freshness of a fish, Connie never bought a herb without establishing that it had been planted when the moon was waxing and picked when it was waning. In the early days, she and her mother were in constant touch through email and then on Skype. Melissa sent Connie complicated instructions for tinctures, bitters, compresses, poultices (and spells, too, I'm pretty certain, although Connie grew evasive when I questioned her on these). About six months after she moved in, I braved the journey down three floors to the big basement kitchen (a smoke alarm had gone off) and found her standing over a pot, waiting for it to simmer.

I was surprised at how different everything looked, even though the furniture and fittings were unchanged. Now the run-down, flag-stoned room had the look of a sorcerer's lair – like a stage set, almost. Labelled jars holding dried roots and leaves filled the shelves of the huge old dresser, and bottles of brandy with herbs seeping in them were lined up in the alcoves on either side of the cooker. The scene was so evocative I wished I could paint it.

'I see why you thought you'd become a medievalist,' I said, 'if you grew up in a kitchen full of weird things in jars and watching your mother stirring concoctions that smell like that one...' I sniffed the air again. 'That pot smells of witch.'

'Doesn't it? It's angelica root. The stuff you said helped your knees.'

The arthritis had started in my knees, and spread within a month to what seemed like every joint in my body. The knees and the fingers looked the worst – the knees hot and swollen, and the fingers of both hands had gradually curved inward and grown rigid, but it was the shoulders that caused the most pain. First the right one went, then the left, and that was the end of sleep. Steroid injections helped for a while, but then they stopped working. I couldn't turn my neck, and after my jaw was affected, I couldn't chew food. I cried a lot and drank even more.

I had pretty well given up hope, but Melissa insisted, with what sounded like genuine conviction, that if I did everything she advised, and took everything Connie gave me, I might notice a turn in only a few weeks. In fact, she was better than her word, because the wickedest pain went almost immediately. This was the lying-still-and-having-done-nothing-to-provoke-it grinding, permanent ache that ran from shoulder to shoulder and through both knees, fed itself off the air, and made sleep hard and waking worse.

On her first day, Connie covered my bed with a heavy plastic, put towels on top of that, put me on top of the towels, covered all the sore joints with a messy, smelly mountain of poultices, and covered the whole lot with a sheet. The pain eased within half an hour. Moving was as painful as ever – making my slow way to the bathroom, I still had the gait of a stiff gorilla, and was dependent on a line of strategically placed chair-backs for support – but then I didn't need to move that much. I had the first long, un-drugged night's sleep that I could remember.

The next morning, we celebrated. My mother travelled up from the basement with a bottle of Champagne and with Nora, the nice elderly Donegal woman – a widow, who lived in Adelaide Road – who came in a few hours a day to do cooking for me. I was glad to see Nora with a Champagne glass in her hand because, like my mother, I had been worrying that Connie's exotic presence in the kitchen might make her uneasy. Nora was a good, honest cook, but had trouble coming to grips with some of the limitations imposed by the illness – not being able to use sunflower oil, for instance, when so many of the television chefs swore by it. She had even more trouble getting out of habits of economy; her faith in margarine, for instance, had been a struggle to break. But Nora's soul was solid.

When she saw that I was nearly purring because of the absence of pain, she started to cry.

'I've prayed for this every night,' she said. 'I was afraid it would never happen. Are you giving her nettles?' she asked Connie suddenly. 'My mother used to swear by nettles.'

Connie confirmed I was getting nettles.

I drank Connie's mysterious – often horrible – potions with increasing interest, and acquired a strange new vocabulary. 'Adaptogen, anti-inflammatory, antimicrobial, lymphatic?' I would inquire. Her oozing compresses and poultices – things I had associated before only with horses – became a 24-hour-a-day part of my increasingly odd world. Perhaps Melissa's most effective advice was that I should keep a gap between me and reality. Never read newspapers or listen to the news; watch comedies, read books with happy endings, and live in a fantasy world with Pat. I did, and it helped. We ate together in the dining room, and went for walks with his old Irish terrier, Seamus, who had died one weekend when I had been forced to go back to hospital briefly. I slept during the day, and read or watched old movies all night.

'Maybe it's a Merrion Square problem,' Connie suggested. 'I read somewhere that Le Fanu never slept before dawn when he was living in number 70 – that he wrote his ghost stories through the night by candlelight.'

And then the thing happened. It was in the middle of week three after Connie's arrival. I had fallen asleep – covered with cheesecloth bags of various herbs and vegetables – in front of a DVD of *Follow the Fleet*, which I had set to keep repeating through the night. I woke, at around four, to Fred and Ginger starting 'Lets Face the Music and Dance' and, almost without noticing, I found I was moving my fingers. I knew it wasn't a dream, even though I went back to sleep almost immediately. The fingers were stiff again in the morning, but I was sure there had been a turn.

For a long time, I assumed I'd never be able to paint again. Not that I was that good at it, but it was the only thing I wanted to do. Then, about two years after Connie's arrival, a portrait I had sweated blood over when I was in my twenties – of a legendary snooker player – came up at an auction in London after his death and sold for about ten times the price I had charged.

That sale, of course, had been a fluke – as indeed had been the original commission. The only reason the legend had asked *me* to paint him back then was because he owned a quarter share of a horse being trained by my mother's father-in-law, who had recommended me; and the recent auction had been a triumph only because the snooker player had just died – prematurely, but not unexpectedly, after a famously misspent life. My portrait of the legend was pretty ordinary – even I could see that – but it was big, which suited the purpose, as it was to hang in a snooker hall named after him. Anyway, the experience made me wonder if I should pull the easel out again.

'Of course you should,' my mother said. 'You won't have a hope of staying healthy if you don't lose yourself in something creative. Even if the joints get a bit strained, that's a minor issue.'

'You're starting to sound like Connie,' I told her, but I knew she was right. Painting did make me feel human again, however small my talent.

I had long ago resigned myself to not having an original thought in my head when I faced a canvas; I was a copycat really. I worked from photographs of the sitters (taken in the hall-floor return – the only room of the house to which 'the public' was given access) and produced portraits in the style of Tamara de Lempicka – but without her flair. Mine were almost comic-book portrayals of individuals, most of them financiers, all against a mildly cubist background representing their work or target of influence. Yet, for some reason, I was surprisingly in demand.

Toby – perhaps as a polite way of making a different point – suggested it might be the depression and bad temper, and even the stiff hands, I brought to the paintings that gave them an unusual edge.

'No, she just hates her subjects,' Connie pronounced. 'And those men' (for some reason, no woman had ever commissioned a portrait from me) 'like it that way.'

'Do you think so?' I asked, having come to the same conclusion myself.

'I'm certain of it. In their world, a black soul is power, and you, for some scary reason, can make those little black souls visible, and they actually like that. Honestly, sometimes I wonder if they might be reincarnations of those 18th century Hellfire Club fellows.'

My mother was inclined to laugh every time she saw one of the finished paintings. 'At least I don't have to worry about whether or not the work is doing you good. There can't possibly be much anger left inside you when you've transferred that kind of fury to a helpless canvas.'

I could see merit in all their views. I neither liked nor understood my clients, but they probably weren't as bad as I made them look. At the time I painted the first of them – an overweight, multi-chinned banker of legend (another connection-by-horse of my mother's invaluable father-in-law) – my right shoulder was hardly functioning, and I made him look so vicious that I half-expected him to throw the finished work back at me. Instead, he was delighted. He was an influential man – a member of that group of financiers and industrialists said to be the real rulers of the world – and with his stamp of approval, I was in demand. Painting the soulless – as Connie described them – became my speciality.

We formed an odd household, particularly after Toby took up residence. He was the smartest of Connie's boyfriends as well as the nicest, and he was certainly a natural fit for the place, being as much removed from the mainstream as Connie and I were. As a student, he had been remarkable. His subject was mathematics, and it had been taken for granted that he would end up as a professor somewhere; but after finishing his PhD (at age 19), he had abandoned that world. His real interest – his passion, in fact – was astrology. He could have made himself rich as an astrologer if he were that way inclined. Somehow his reputation had spread (he had worked briefly for a bookmaker after he decided to stay in Dublin – Connie thought that might be the explanation); and like me, he was a magnet for dead-eyed men in suits. They turned up at the house sometimes – no one knew how they had got the address – offering him large sums of money for his advice. Unlike me, he always turned them away.

He was the first of Connie's boyfriends who moved in with her. She had proposed that he might – very tentatively – when she saw how much I liked him. 'Just for a few weeks, to try it out, and I promise he won't bother you.'

I agreed – reluctantly – only because I didn't want to risk losing Connie. Within a week I was glad I had, when Connie ended up in hospital for a few days after an accident (a drunk cyclist had run into her on the Dawson Street pavement, and she hit her head when she fell) at the same time as Nora was out of action with a bad cold. That happened in November, when I was at my stiffest. Toby took a few days off from his restaurant job, cooked meals in the attic kitchen, brought endless cups of tea, and watched old movies with me.

It was while she was in the hospital that Connie met Bea, who was her night nurse. On her last evening, Connie had asked Toby to bring in a box of chocolates for Bea, and when Connie presented it, Bea started to cry and left the room. When they asked another nurse if she was all right, she told them that Bea and her husband were losing their flat the following week. It was part of a house that had been repossessed by a bank, and the bank had given eviction notices to all the tenants, none of whom had been able to find another flat they could afford. Connie had telephoned me from the hospital. 'Do you think they could stay in Charlie's rooms just for the moment – while Toby and I help them find a place?'

'I suppose so,' I said cautiously. 'Is she nice?'

'She's awfully nice. But listen to this. Her husband's a builder, but he can't get a work permit here.'

His occupation settled it, as Connie must have guessed it would. That was six years ago. Now I was in dread of the day I might lose them. Paul and Bea seemed to be happy enough with the arrangement too; every year, on the anniversary of the day they moved in, they had a Mass said for my intentions.

The 'Charlie' to whom Connie was referring (and to whom I had been dreaming of finding a successor) had been caretaker of the house for the previous owner. He was dead for nearly 30 years, but everyone felt they knew him personally because of the wonderful portrait of him, done by my aunt, which hung in the entrance hall. It showed a smiling, thin, almost toothless old man with bent shoulders, holding on his lap a dog that looked as happy as it was un-groomed – a West Highland terrier with its matted white fur almost black from the smoke-filled air of 1970s Dublin.

My Aunt Betsy, my mother's sister, had got to know Charlie when she was 18. He was about sixty then, from the country, and in his past life, had been 'a cattle drover,' he told her – whatever that was. As the caretaker of a house in flats, he lived in the basement and did pottering sorts of jobs for the tenants: putting out the rubbish, taking in deliveries, sweeping the stairs, changing fuses.

My aunt was from the country, too, from a farm in Kerry. She had come to Dublin to study at the National College of Art, where she was regarded, my grandmother told me, as particularly talented – by one instructor anyway –

but about as lazy a student as had ever attended the place. My aunt's explanation was that she was distracted by city life – her first taste of it ever. She found the course interesting enough, but the freedom to explore endless streets and shops got the better of her. She had a particular obsession with Dublin's Georgian terraces, the result of an adolescence passed contentedly with Georgette Heyer novels. She came to know Merrion Square better than any of the others because of the little dog, Topsy, who spent her days in the area outside the open basement door of the house my aunt would later live in, and where I was living now. My aunt always stopped to talk to Topsy, and that was how she got to know Topsy's owner, Charlie.

The flats in the house of which Charlie was caretaker were of a type much coveted back then, when the law still gave their long-term tenants both rent control and a right of possession. There was one flat to each floor, and all the tenants were women, the youngest in her late fifties. According to Charlie, there was one nice tenant – the actress who had the first-floor flat, which took in the original drawing room of the house. The other three, he thought grumpy and stand-offish, particularly the retired civil servant who lived in the hall-floor flat, which had the house's original dining room.

When my aunt graduated and (to everyone's surprise) took a job as a fashion buyer for a department store, she saw even more of Charlie and Topsy; and when Charlie had a minor stroke and was out of action for a while, my aunt minded Topsy.

When Charlie heard from the actress on the first floor that the grumpy ex-civil-servant on the hall floor was about to vacate her flat to move into a care home, he rang my aunt at work to tell her to get on to the landlord immediately, and then he told the landlord about my aunt.

The upshot was that, at age twenty-three, my aunt found herself in possession of two very large, very grand, very cold, and pretty well 'original condition' rooms on the hall floor of a house in Merrion Square (plus a dingy kitchen and dingier bathroom in the hall-floor return, reached through the communal hallway). It was so much a dream come true that she thought her life had peaked too soon: what remained for her to aspire to?

As a tenant, she was a landlord's fantasy. While the other women who lived in the house were agitating, unsuccessfully, for better plumbing and the installation of some rudimentary heating, my aunt was asking for permission to redecorate the glorious bow-ended dining room with a misty, delicately coloured, highly romanticized, and slightly Italianate mural of Killarney's lakes in the early 19th century (with history altered by a barely visible United Irishmen's flag flying on Ross Castle). Her most triumphant moment came on an off-day in an auction room on the Quays when she was the only bidder for a three-pillar Georgian dining table, and then for a dozen chairs, all from around 1790. When extended, the table might seat twenty (sixteen in comfort) if anyone had that many chairs; and, unusually, it had all its original leaves. It became famous within the family when an insurance valuer was so astonished at what he saw in the dining room that he called in a specialist to confirm his opinion. The specialist must have agreed with him, because my aunt's premium shot up, and she had to borrow money from my grandparents to cover that year's insurance.

My mother was three years older than Aunt Betsy. She had studied at the School of Art in Cork, but almost immediately after she graduated, married a neighbouring farmer she had known all her life. They had been trying to have a baby for six years when I arrived. Six years later, she was widowed; a tractor my father was driving had overturned. Our farm was only a few miles from her parents' farm, and she moved back in with them after the death and they took care of things for her, selling off stock and renting out the land. She put on the best face she could when I was around, but the nights were bad for her.

Sometimes I wondered did she ever sleep. She cried at night and I used to crawl into her bed. My grandparents did everything they could, pampering and cosseting the two of us so relentlessly that I sometimes wonder how I was ever able to cope with the world afterwards – or perhaps I never was able really, and that's the explanation.

One Sunday, as a treat, when I was ten, they brought us to lunch at a new hotel that had opened nearby and that all the neighbours were talking about. My grandfather gamely swallowed his principles for the outing. The hotel was in a converted country house. ('A Cromwell place,' he had always called it, 'built with the bones of murdered Irish – it might as well have been anyway. I don't even like looking at it'.)

An Englishman travelling on his own was seated at the table next to ours. My grandfather recognized him. He was a racing commentator, and his father had trained a Grand National winner. My grandfather seemed to know every horse his father had trained, and my mother and grandmother couldn't stop him talking about them. The man came back with us to the house afterwards for a visit. Then he became a regular visitor. His name was Jasper, and although he was a nice, funny, generous man, I used to hate when he visited because of the way my mother acted when he was around. She hadn't liked company since my father died, but she liked it fine when Jasper was there.

He was divorced and had twin daughters a year older than I was. They came on a visit with him once and the three of us hardly spoke. None of us had any welcome for the changed future that was opening up before our eyes.

My mother and Aunt Betsy owned another farm between them, near Killarney – one they had inherited from an unmarried uncle. When the law controlling rented dwellings was changed so that Betsy and other protected tenants no longer had rights, my mother suggested the two of them should offer to buy the Merrion Square house. The farmer who rented their uncle's land had been pressing them for years to sell it to him, and Dublin house prices had plummeted, so they might be lucky. They were – eventually. The owner of the Merrion Square house was a nice man, now nearly 80; his father had converted the house to flats – then very exclusive ones – in the 1930s. He wasn't that eager to sell that house at first, although he had sold a few of his other properties; but they kept asking, and finally he agreed.

My grandparents worried that lawyers would help themselves to the money my mother and aunt were paid for the Killarney farm; they'd seen it happen too many times before, particularly when a property was left to just women – but Jasper helped. He said they should set up a trust, which they did, and he said his own lawyer (an elderly man who could be relied on because he owned two horses being trained by his father and wasn't likely to put that arrangement at risk) would keep an eye on the contract.

My grandfather had other reservations about buying in Merrion Square. He disliked its history. 'I don't see how any luck can come out of one of those houses. Who built it anyway, the one you're buying? It wasn't put up for the natives – that's for certain.'

My aunt giggled. 'I don't think they even let them in as servants in the beginning.'

'Do you know whose house it was?' my grandmother asked.

'Well, the first owner was Lord something or other, who moved on after the Act of Union, and the second owner was notorious – a hanging-drawing-and-quartering judge. But what can you do if you want a pretty house in the centre of Dublin? – they all have that kind of history. There was Robert Emmett's house on Stephen's Green, of course. That would have been a nice one to buy, but that's the one they decided to demolish.'

'Charlie says he knows people down the country who

had their house cleansed when they thought there were bad spirits in it,' my mother said. 'An old man went through all the rooms doing something. We could do that.'

After the deal went through, Charlie's man came to Merrion Square. When he had finished his mysterious work and the four of them were having tea, my aunt declared, 'I intend to die in this house.'

In fact, she would die in Switzerland twenty years later. She was on a walking holiday with two other women. Her death was unexpected. It seemed she had the sort of heart condition that people have a pacemaker fitted for, but the weakness had never been detected. 'It was a good death,' a nice Swiss doctor told us. 'Her heart, it just stopped. She would not have known anything.'

I couldn't stop crying when I heard the news, and was terrified for my mother, knowing how close she had been to Betsy. My mother, however, took the death better than I did.

'The truth is,' she said, 'I was prepared for it – I had the oddest experience just before it happened. I had woken up with these exact words in my head: "Betsy's going to die and there's nothing you can do about it." It wasn't that I heard a voice exactly, but those were the precise words – just in my head. I even phoned her hotel in Switzerland to check if she was all right, and she was grand. I didn't tell you at the time because it was one of those things you can't believe mean anything until – well, until it's happened.'

I had been sharing the Merrion Square house with Aunt Betsy for years before her death – from the time I, in my turn, was a lazy art student in Dublin. My rooms were on the top floor, where Connie and Toby were now. The elderly tenants were long dead by then, and so was Charlie, and the house had settled into a pretty good compromise between comfort and 18th century purity. My aunt had brought back to almost-museum standard all the original reception rooms on the hall floor and first floor, but on the two floors above, she had left the kitchenettes and bathrooms in the locations where they had been installed in the 1930s, but with new fittings. The truth was that, even if they would have won no conservation award, they made living in the house so comfortable it was hard to dismantle them.

On the main bedroom floor, it was the bow-ended back bedroom that had been divided up, but even after the small kitchen and bathroom had been taken out of it, a decent-sized sitting room remained with an interestingly odd fire surround – a bit smoke-stained, with a pattern of a vine carved into the white marble of its top and sides, and the slight scale of which was a better match for the reduced-size room than it would have been for the full space. Back in the thirties, a plaster cornice matching the original had been put up around the partitions, which had made the sub-division gentler on the eye. Aunt Betsy had made this her winter bedroom, and for me, it was bedroom, sitting room, and pretty well my whole world after I came out of hospital. It was warm and convenient, and for exercise, I could do repeated hobbles – ghost-like, hair uncombed, and in my nightdress – through the front bedroom (a huge space that had been two large bedrooms in its days as a flat) overlooking the Square.

Often I sat in the dark in that big front room sipping a cup of tea or a glass of wine and staring out one of its windows. In Aunt Betsy's years as a tenant, in the seventies and early eighties, and particularly before the railed-in garden was opened to the public, the Square was a quiet, dark place at night. There were a few streetwalkers, but not as many as in nearby Fitzwilliam Square or in the terraces along the canal. On all four sides, there were still some flats, furnished ones mostly, often on the top floor, a world, as she pictured it, of sagging beds, mismatched veneers, drawers that stuck, chairs that wobbled, exposed pipes, alarming geysers, and ancient lino-ends – all trademarks back then of furnished Georgian flatland. My aunt used to identify the flats by their hanging incandescent bulbs.

'I wonder why it is that flats are so much more intriguing than houses,' she said to my mother one winter evening when the air smelled of coal smoke and the two of them were sitting at a second-floor window, sharing a bottle of wine and looking out at those dim spots of light. 'I can drive past miles of houses in the suburbs and never have a thought about who lives in any of them. I couldn't imagine spending evening after evening speculating about what's going on behind their windows.'

'Maybe it's just these flats,' my mother suggested. 'The Georgian flats, I mean. Even the crudest of them come with ghosts, and they're such private places. There could be anyone in them doing anything. That sort of posh murderer they arrested in the Attorney General's apartment – he'd lived in a flat in Upper Mount Street for a while.'

But now there were no tenants to speak of and those windows were nearly all dark. In my time, the Square garden had become a municipal park, often bedlam at weekends, but closed at night except to the more enterprising homeless.

When I was young, my friends used to love visiting Merrion Square. Sometimes I wished I were less my grandfather's grandchild, and could see the Square through their eyes. We all thought the houses were beautiful, but I was never able to find their history romantic, the way my friends did. Some of their non-original residents were interesting all right – Oscar Wilde and W. B. Yeats and Daniel O'Connell – but my grandfather's strong feeling that those houses were built during and with the proceeds of a period of horror never fully left me, and when I was most depressed, became almost too much for me. Sitting at the window in the dark for too long, my mind never saw well-dressed strollers in the park or elegant carriages. All it saw was a vision of hell on the street below, near-naked beggars and elaborately uniformed soldiers. On the worst nights, I wondered if the man my aunt and mother had got to cleanse the house had really done his job.

After I was settled in Dublin as a student, my mother married Jasper and moved to England. His daughters and their mother had moved to New York, which made the decision easier for her. Before my mother committed herself, she asked me if I minded, but by then, I was delighted. Not only did I really like Jasper, but I felt a surprising sense of release – I hadn't known until then how much I used to worry about my mother, even when my grandparents were alive. Since they had died, I used never go to sleep at night without wondering about her, but now Jasper had taken that weight from me.

She and Jasper often came to stay in Merrion Square – always in the basement rooms my aunt had fixed for Charlie, who was nearly eighty and very frail by the time she and my mother bought the house. 'The only two warm rooms in Ireland,' Jasper always said of them. The big old kitchen was so formidable in its requirements that my aunt had done no more than re-wire and re-plumb it, but the two bedrooms in the basement had been dried and insulated on every surface so that the fragile Charlie, could heat them by the proverbial light bulb. When Bea and Paul moved into them, they told me gratefully that it was the first time they had been warm since they arrived from the Philippines.

At the time Aunt Betsy died, I was engaged to Pat, who was a veterinarian. Both she and my mother had pushed me to get engaged to him. 'Grab him, for heaven's sake,' Aunt Betsy said one night, after she came back from a leaden party in the suburbs with some co-workers. 'For an only child raised in *South* Dublin by *those* parents to have emerged without a pompous bone in his body – his soul has passed a great test. You'd be foolish to let him slip away.'

The plan at first – his plan, anyway – was that we

would take up residence in his house in Monkstown. I hated the idea of living in the suburbs, but his house had a huge garden and he didn't want to be short of space for animals.

After Aunt Betsy's death, Pat was wondering if my mother planned to sell the Merrion Square house; but now that Aunt Betsy was gone, I couldn't bear the idea of leaving it. I tried to convince Pat that the two of us should move in there. 'There's *some* open space at the back,' I pointed out, 'and the walls are really high, which is good. Anyway, dogs always prefer being in the house, and you can't deny that there's plenty of space in there.'

'Invite his parents to dinner,' my mother suggested. 'Do the grandest dinner you can in the dining room. Pat won't notice much, but you want to impress his mother. Don't cook yourself, whatever you do. I'll pay for a cook for the night – you just find one. Use plenty of candles and every bit of the old crystal that Betsy picked up.'

I have no idea whether or not it was the dinner that did it, but afterwards Pat agreed to rent out the Monkstown house and move into Merrion Square.

We planned to do work on the house before the wedding – on the old basement kitchen, in particular – but ran out of time. We were so busy we didn't even unpack our presents. The boxes, many of them marked china, crystal, silver, were stored in the dining room, most with wedding paper still around them.

For our honeymoon, we went to Africa and looked at wildlife. A lot of wildlife. It wasn't one of the luxurious safaris that have a five-star tent as a base; it was 'authentic'. We spent the nights in a sort of a van. At times, it was fascinating, but I wouldn't have minded a grand hotel room or two in the mix. Pat, however, thought it was the holiday of his life. It was my concession to him – a bloody big one, I thought – for his agreeing to move into the Merrion Square house.

When we arrived back in Dublin, we got into his car

at the airport, drove tiredly as far as the motorway, and then, unbelievably, another car came racing at us in the wrong direction. Six teenage joyriders were packed into it. Two of them were killed and Pat was killed. I had a lot of broken bones, but nothing I wouldn't recover from in time. The bigger problem was that I developed severe rheumatoid arthritis. 'We've seen it before,' the doctors told me. 'A major stress just hits some people that way.'

'So, where are we having my great birthday dinner?' I asked Bea and Connie, remembering all those unpacked boxes.

'In the dining room,' Connie answered uneasily, as Bea put an arm around me.

It was an awkward moment for everyone. I said nothing at first, while both girls looked at me nervously. That room was a subject we never spoke about. I hadn't been inside it for ten years. The door that led to it from the hall had not been opened, in my presence, in all that time. Nothing rational had kept me away from it: just a problem inside the head of the damaged replica of myself that had been born the night Pat died. The dining room had been more than that sorry creature could cope with. After life turned bad, its memories and its unopened presents made it a place to stay away from – a museum of vanished normality.

'But what about all the stuff in it?' I asked.

'We unpacked your wedding presents,' Connie answered.

'Your mother asked us to,' Bea added quickly. 'We wouldn't have disturbed them if she hadn't asked.'

'We've been doing nothing but polishing and washing for the last week. Do you have any idea how much silver, crystal, and china you have?'

'A lot, I guess,' I answered absentmindedly. 'Everyone gave us that stuff as wedding presents. It was because of the dining room – Aunt Betsy's murals and table and everything.'

Connie and Bea looked at one another – probably wondering how to interpret the dull calm with which I was taking the news. I wasn't sure what to make of it myself. Since Pat's death, I had thought it would be a desecration to empty those boxes, but now that it had happened, I felt more relief than anything else – finally I didn't have to think about them anymore.

'Well, it's about time,' I said at last, and then laughed. 'Lord, that did sound strange – as if I've been possessed by some half-normal person – maybe it's the dress.'

'By dinnertime, you're even going to *look* normal,' Connie said. 'There's a hairdresser coming to the house, and…'

'What?' Even I was surprised at how sharp my voice sounded.

'Your mother's arranged it,' Bea said hurriedly. 'She's been planning this a long time. She's gone to so much trouble. It will be very nice,' she added with a plea in her voice.

'Look, you can't go to your own party looking like you do now,' Connie said. 'We knew you'd never go out to a hairdresser, so that's why we arranged for one to come here.'

Bea was tweaking Connie's sleeve. It was obvious there was more, but Bea was afraid to say it. 'And there's a facialist coming as well,' Connie said at last.

'A what?' I said again.

'That's what they call them. It's someone who…'

'I can guess what it is. But what's one of them doing coming here?'

'Look, it's going to be fine,' Connie said reassuringly, taking the lid off a box she had rested on the bed. It was filled with small bottles containing a dark liquid. 'I even have a potion for you to take every hour on the hour. This is the stuff they gave to Russian cosmonauts to survive space, so it should carry you through a bit of tidying up and a dinner.'

'We have naps scheduled too,' Bea added in a tiny voice. 'Your mother said we should. This party is very important for her.' The plea was even more audible.

'There's just no choice,' Connie said. 'For any of us. Your mother and Jasper will be here at seven, and we have to make sure you're primped, painted, and corseted before then. If we help you take all that stuff off now, you'll have time to breathe in the meantime.'

It was an arduous day. I have heard the experience I was put through described as pampering – I have no idea why. My ordinary days had far more to do with pampering. Going to bed when I liked, getting up when I liked, a quick shower, never looking in a mirror, spending the day in a bathrobe if I wanted. It was only because I knew that Connie was right about there being no way out that I resigned myself – sulkily – to what was ahead.

The facialist came first – a skilful Slovenian my mother had heard could work miracles. The woman was booked for an hour but stayed for an hour and a half, trying to de-puff the eyes. 'I should have been called in a month ago,' she kept saying in frustration. 'Or at least a week ago. Then I could have made a difference.'

In fact, she accomplished an awful lot. She might not have got the eyes back to normal, but she got them to within the range of normal, which was a place they hadn't been for many years. I was allowed half an hour to rest before the hairdresser arrived: a bright, pregnant girl named Jasmine who had worked up to recently at one of Dublin's posher hair salons, but had given up that job temporarily because of the chemicals, and now was doing hairdressing for the patients at Bea's hospital.

Jasmine was used to dealing with sick people. She came with a special chair and with plastic constructions to put over the bathroom basin, and she was skilful and careful about my neck, but I still found it hard to imagine in advance that the result could be worth the trouble. What she achieved, however, surprised everyone. The colouring was perfect, and the trimming and styling were transformational. She gave me a pageboy cut to match the dress, but which fell cleverly around the face in a way that distracted from the eye bags a bit more.

When she was finished, I napped again, until Connie shook me awake, handing me one of her bottles of potion to drink – the fifth of the day. 'You should probably start on your make-up now,' she suggested. 'In case it takes a while.'

I did make a start, but discovered pretty quickly that I had forgotten what to do. I remembered I used to dilute a foundation with something, although I'd forgotten with what – some moisturiser, I imagined – but it was academic anyway as the foundation had separated with age, and the ancient jars of moisturiser smelled when I looked into them. The mascara had gone hard, and although the eye pencils looked ok, Bea was worried I might get an infection if I used them. Connie said she'd grab a taxi and get replacements, and it all worked out fine because I had a chance to lie down and sleep for a full hour. I woke up feeling human again.

'Grooming is a total bitch,' I said to Bea when she brought me a cup of tea after Connie had come back weighted down with a heavy bag of make-up. 'I can see why I don't bother with it any more.'

'Oh no,' she said with an intensity that surprised me. 'You must stay this way now. Your mother is very worried.'

'Worried? Why do you say that?'

'Because you look a holy show,' Connie said quickly. 'That's why I bought so much concealer.'

In the end, Connie helped me with the make-up, saying I wasn't using a heavy enough hand. 'The girl in the shop showed me how to layer it up,' she said.

When she had finished, I couldn't stop looking at myself in the mirror. 'They look just normal black circles now, don't they?'

'You look really good,' Connie said, unable to keep

the surprise out of her voice. 'Your mother's going to be thrilled.'

'Was this party all her idea?'

Connie nodded. 'But of course we all thought it was a great one. I warned her she'd better come properly dressed herself. No jeans for once.'

'And she definitely hasn't invited anyone else?'

'No, don't worry. She was wondering in the beginning about inviting some of the people you and Pat knew –'

When I jumped, she pressed my shoulder reassuringly. 'But she would have checked with you first. Anyway, she decided against it. She was worried it would do more harm than good.'

'Thank God for that.'

'She said forty was a mean age. Your friends would all be struggling with school fees and trying to buy bigger houses, and they'd look around these huge grand rooms and hate you.'

'She's probably right. And I don't want to see *them* because I look like a corpse that's been dug up, and they're probably all gleaming with health and talking about their dozens of children.'

'Well, you look knock-dead glamorous right now,' Connie said.

'At least my mother's wised-up, even if she is an old hippie. When she and my aunt bought this place, they did it through a trust, and they never let on afterwards that they owned it. They'd probably have lost every friend they had if people did know. You know what Dublin's like.'

'Do you know, Sasha, the waiter, has only one eye?' Connie said suddenly. 'Toby wanted to have the house lit just by candlelight tonight – except in the kitchen, of course. There we had to install extra super-duper lighting for Remy, who had the same opinion of your light bulb dangling from the middle of the ceiling as he had of your cooker. But with Sasha's one eye, we thought we'd better leave a normal level of light on the route from the kitchen to the dining room, so electricity's allowed there.'

I giggled. 'Okay.'

'But it's only candlelight and firelight everywhere else, so you'll have to watch yourself in those heels. Bea or I will go up and down the stairs with you, and don't forget to hold tight to the handrail.'

By seven, we were all in the first-floor front drawing room, waiting for my mother and Jasper. We were a smug little group. 'What is it about evening dress?' Connie asked. 'Do you think even cocaine can make you feel more arrogant?'

Like everyone else, I couldn't stop looking in the mirror; but to be fair to ourselves, we did make a dramatic picture. Connie's dress (bought from the same vintage shop as mine) was from the 1930s – pink, floor-length, and bias-cut. Bea's beautiful dress was from the Philippines – bright red, also floor-length, and with butterfly sleeves; and Paul wore an elegant embroidered shirt he called a barong. Toby was in white tie and tails. 'Borrowed it all from a friend who's in the concert orchestra,' he explained. 'He's not playing tonight.'

There was a roaring fire, serviced by a slight young man who slipped silently in every fifteen minutes to add logs and turf, and then slipped out again. 'His name's Ernest,' Toby whispered to me. 'He's a philosophy student. He's supposed to be very smart, but he talks even less than Paul. He plays the piano on Saturday nights at Remy's.'

Toby had mixed martinis – in honour of my dress – and was pouring them into vintage cocktail glasses that I remembered being part of Aunt Betsy's vast collection. I was relieved he wasn't using new glasses – ones that might have been some wedding present I knew nothing about. I hoped to heaven the dinner would be served on her china too, rather than on some set that had just been unpacked. She had so much, I told myself, it probably would be. Whatever happened, I wouldn't let on.

We were clustered at one of the front windows watching a fox family of a vixen and two cubs strolling proprietorially along the pavement when Paul spotted my mother and Jasper, and ran down to open the door. I tried to follow, but Connie held me back.

'You're going nowhere,' she said. 'You're our Eliza Doolittle. We want to see their expressions when they get a first glimpse of you.'

In fact, my mother did look for a moment as if she might burst into tears when she came through the door, although her first words were not overly sentimental. 'You should pull down the blinds, Maud. You all look so beautiful – every one of you – you're making far too spectacular a show to the street.'

'*We* look beautiful! Just look at the two of you!' I said, as they handed to Toby the overcoats they had worn on the short walk from the hotel. Jasper was in black tie, which I hadn't seen him wear before, and my mother – my makeup-hating, jeans-wearing mother – was almost unrecognizable.

She had never – in my lifetime anyway – been to a hairdresser, but obviously she had been to one that day. She had a dramatic bit of fringe on one side which was new, and it suited her. Her hair had been swept back behind her ears, from which long Art Deco earrings dangled, and her dress – well, it was floor-length, black, and I swear it was a Lanvin. I had never known her to spend money on clothes, but tonight... 'You look sensational,' I told her.

'Thanks Maud, but to tell the truth, the duds didn't seem too appropriate on the walk here. I couldn't get over all the homeless. We passed more than a dozen of them just between the hotel and the front door. There was one old woman at the corner who didn't even have a coat. Could you...?'

'I'll run out with a couple of blankets for her,' Toby said quickly. 'And a fleece jacket. And I'll cadge a cup of soup or something hot off Sasha.'

'We keep a stack of blankets and stuff to give out,' I explained. 'But you have no idea how bad it really is. Just wait until you look out the windows later tonight. You'll see all these odd little flickers of light in the bushes. A lot of the homeless sleep in the Square now. They hide in the bushes until after dark or else they climb over the railings somehow. It really seems post-nuclear at times, except when the city puts on those bedlammy events at weekends.'

'It used to be silent as a tomb at weekends,' my mother said. 'When Betsy first moved into the Square, she said the whole area around here was so deserted on Sundays – Sunday afternoons, in particular – that she worried sometimes about walking out on her own. Once two men in a van slowed up beside her and she got such a fright she ended up pushing on a strange doorbell.'

'Well, it's different now. If you'd been here last Sunday... But the soundproofing does take the edge off it.'

In my back bedroom I had done some sneaky work on the windows. Thanks to new glass, and to the skills of Paul and a few of his silent, ingenious Asian friends, no one would ever see any changes, but the room now had the equivalent of triple glazing. In the first lawless act of my life, I hadn't applied for planning permission; maybe the planners would have been fine, but then maybe not. The house was where I spent my days and nights, and I wasn't taking any chance with officialdom.

'Now I can just retreat to the bedroom when they have those things going on in the Square. I have CDs of harp music that I put on for white noise, and it's not that bad.'

'Talk about fogies,' Connie said, topping my martini. 'Yes, folks, she did say harp music.'

Most of us, except Bea and Paul who were teetotallers, were already half-drunk when the philosophy student came to ask us to go downstairs. He had tended the dining room just before summoning us, and the fire in the grate was roaring. Candle-holders of varying height and formality rested on every horizontal surface in the room, the grandest of them on the mantelpiece and on the famous table. In the flickering light produced by the mix of fire and candle, the room looked extraordinary – even more dramatic and lost in time than I remembered. But the eerie power I imagined it had over me – well, that was real, and I felt it then. When I walked through the door, the past came at me with such a rush that it might have ruffled the chiffon of my dress.

'It is full of ghosts,' Connie said, looking at me. 'We all feel it.'

'Well it looks spectacular,' I said at last. 'You did a heroic job.'

Toby, as a further homage to *Rear Window*, had suggested lobster for the main course, but that had been vetoed by Connie and Bea, the usually mild Bea having declared with passion that she could never again eat in the kitchen if live lobsters were thrown into boiling water there.

One triumphant concession to 1950s style, however, was a monster tin of Beluga caviar provided by Jasper, a gift from a Russian billionaire whose string of winning horses he had written about. The Ukrainian waiter, Sasha – an even more dramatic presence than I expected because of his great height and expressionless face as well as his eye patch – placed the caviar, in its tin, on a mound of crushed ice in the middle of the table; and we ate it with mother-of-pearl spoons, also provided by the billionaire. 'It's some kind of mogul thing,' Jasper explained, as we all admired them. 'You can't be in the club if you don't eat Beluga with mother-of-pearl spoons.'

At about four in the morning, while the party was still in full swing, I felt so tired that I decided to go upstairs to lie down for a few minutes, and my mother came with me. We left behind a noisy room. Toby had produced a stack of ancient sheet music which the actress tenant had left behind, and which I had stored in the attic. Somewhere in the pile, Jasper found 'Love's Old Sweet

Song,' and while Ernest played it on the baby grand in the back drawing room, Jasper and Toby sang the lyrics at the top of their voices. Connie and Paul were trying to dance, but having trouble getting the rhythm. Bea was stretched out on a sofa, giggling helplessly.

We were planning to get back to the party after a quarter of an hour or so, but the moment I touched the bed, I fell asleep, and then my mother fell asleep beside me, both of us in our full party gear.

She and Jasper had checked into the hotel that was beside the Square (or the Duke of Wellington's house, as my grandfather had always called it with a snarl – 'they didn't demolish that one, did they?'). Some time after dawn, Paul and Toby walked Jasper back to it, but there was a consensus that my mother and I shouldn't be disturbed.

Toby woke us with a pot of tea at eleven o'clock, saying we were the most decadent-looking pair he had ever seen. 'Give a shout if you want more tea or Champagne or anything. Or if you want Connie to help you off with your dresses. It was a great night, wasn't it?'

My mother did swap her dress for a bathrobe before settling into the tea, but I kept mine on. 'You should wear eye make-up more often,' I told her. 'It looks very dramatic this morning. The black has smeared, and you look…'

'I know exactly what I look like,' she said laughing. 'Yours has gone the same way, and I was thinking how much it suited you. But tell me how did you manage to fall asleep in that corset? Won't you hurt yourself leaving it on longer?'

'Probably. But I can't bear to take the dress off. I'll breathe later.'

She looked in the direction of her own gown, now hanging in the wardrobe. 'You know, I'm 67, and that's the first grown-up dress I've ever bought for myself.'

'Did you buy it for last night?'

'No, but this was my chance to enjoy it. It's one of the outfits I'll be wearing for Goneril's wedding in New York. That wretched affair is going to go on for three days.'

'You poor thing. I thought you weren't going.'

'Well, I didn't plan to. But I have to really – for Jasper's sake.'

Goneril was one of Jasper's daughters. Her real name was Emma and her twin's name was Sarah, but my mother and I had never called them anything Goneril and Regan.

'Goneril's going to hate you,' I said happily. 'Have you bought other outfits?'

'Lots of them. I went a bit mad, to be honest, but I felt like I was buying armour. You know how Goneril and her mother are.'

'Well, at least you'll be travelling again. You haven't made a real trip in ages. I can't even remember the last time you went with Jasper to any of those glamorous race places. I'm amazed you let him go to Hong Kong so often without you.'

'So am I,' she said, and was silent for a while. 'The truth is,' she said then, with a note of unease in her voice that made me turn to look at her, 'I haven't felt that comfortable travelling since you got sick. Every time I got on an airplane, I'd worry in case it crashed, and then what would happen to you?'

'You don't mean that, do you?' I asked, astonished. 'I'm forty, remember, and very nicely set up compared to most. You don't need to take me into account at all now when you want to do anything. I'd feel terrible if you did.'

'Maud, you haven't had a normal day since Pat died. I worry about you all the time.'

'But I'm perfectly happy. I know I lead an odd life, but...'

'Well, I'm not worried because it's odd, but in your case, I think it's dangerous.'

When she said that, I laughed. 'Honestly, I think I lead about the least dangerous...'

'No, it is dangerous. You're not living in the real world. While I'm around, you have a safety net, and at the moment you're surrounded by nice trustworthy people, but what will you do when they move on? And they're bound to. Toby and Connie are a bit too large to be contained by Dublin for much longer, and Paul and Bea might not be able to stay here indefinitely – when you think of the problems poor Paul's had already. Of course they're all so contented here,' she added laughing, 'you may never get rid of any of them, but...'

'And I'm contented too. And honestly...how many people do you know who are totally contented?'

'Well, of people age forty, none at all. But I'd sleep a lot better if you were a bit independent as well. When I wake in the middle of the night, which I do all the time now, I keep thinking how you haven't even been out to a shop once since before you were married. Or to a bank. Or to a dinner party. You've hardly walked on a pavement since then, have you?'

'And how much have I missed? Shops? Banks? Remember, I'd given up shopping in Grafton Street long before I was married. All those creepy security men stalking me for some reason.'

She laughed. 'Yes, I'd forgotten how bad they are. I had one following me today. Connie told me she did too when she was buying your make-up.'

'But I will grant you,' I said, unable to stop playing with the huge chiffon skirt as I was talking, 'it was a lot of fun dressing up again, even though the preparations damn near killed me. In fact, you know what would be really great – if you could come back here for your birthday. I know it would be pretty hot on the heels of Goneril's wedding, but it would be fun. Connie knows two girls who cater dinner parties. It wouldn't be the same as having Remy and Sasha, of course, but we could wear our dresses again. I could clear the big bedroom for the two of you.'

'Oh, I'd love that, Maud,' she said eagerly, but then hesitated. 'I don't suppose there's any chance,' she said finally, 'that you'd be willing to invite some outsiders for that dinner – just to show you can do it?'

'No. I don't want any bloody outsiders.'

My voice was sharper than I intended, but my mother just laughed. 'All right then. No outsiders.'

I like things fine the way they are.'

'Well, I understand that,' she said easily. 'Remember, I was a bit like that once. I wasn't exactly eager for company after your father died. And his family – well, you remember what they were like. I don't think they ever forgave us for inheriting the farm. Even that day we met Jasper – I was ready to murder Daddy for inviting him back to the house. But look how it's turned out – I'm having a great life in my old age. Apart from worrying about you.'

'Do you know when I really got tired of people? It was after I came out of hospital and then had to go back again, and I had to share a room with that horrible woman from...oh, I don't know. From somewhere in Wicklow, I think. Pat's will had just appeared in the list in the Sunday paper and it seemed like he'd left a lot of money because of the insurance, and because his house was valued so high with that huge garden. That dreadful woman knew Pat's family, so she knew a bit about me, and she actually *asked* me how much compensation I was getting from the crash, and she kept talking about how *lucky* I was. And that was the weekend that Seamus died – in a kennel! Pat's mother had put him in a kennel while I was in hospital.'

'They didn't want to, really. They had to go away suddenly. They were as upset about Seamus as you were.'

'He shouldn't have been put in a kennel,' I said. I could never keep my voice calm when I talked about Seamus.

'Of course not,' she said soothingly. 'And to tell you the truth, I've never been able to forgive myself for not coming to Dublin that weekend so he could have stayed here. I had that wretched virus, but I could still have travelled. I was just afraid you'd catch it. He was such a smart old dog.' She looked over at the walnut dressing table with the two silver-framed photographs. 'That's a nice photo of him. It's bigger than the one of Pat.'

I giggled. 'I know. It was Pat who framed it.'

'But there are nice people out there, Maud. I know they're not in the majority, but there are some, and you won't meet them if you don't...'

'Sometimes I wonder how well even Pat and I would have got on after I got sick – I mean, I know I probably wouldn't have got sick if he were alive and if we'd never had that crash – but if I had. It's such a grotty, boring illness when nothing much works on it, and although he was great at sick animals – well, who knows. I mean, I'm not a burden on anyone at the moment. That's the best part of the way things are here – we're all living in an arrangement of mutual advantage, and for anyone who has a tiresome sickness, it's pretty much a miracle to land on a situation like that.'

'But you're only forty, Maud. Yesterday, you were only thirty-nine, for heaven's sake. Do you have any idea how young that is? And I admit that Goneril's wedding is making me jealous, but why wouldn't it? She's a year older than you are, and she's horrible.'

'You can't really be thinking that I'd get married again?' I said, startled. 'That honestly is not going to happen. If I ever even thought about it – and I don't – just think of the miserable pool of eligibles I'd find out there at age forty – or even age thirty-nine, for that matter.'

'A lot of very nice men are slow to get married. They're shy.'

'And if I were lonely, I might find that interesting. Then, who knows, maybe even the indignity of working my way through every untrustworthy, treacherous, and mercenary hopeful left standing, just on the chance I'd

land on some pearl of solidity who wasn't even more stuck
in his ways than I am, would seem worthwhile. But the
thing is, I'm not lonely. Even shut in here, I see more than
I want of the world. I see the homeless out there hiding
in the bushes, and I see all too clearly the moguls who
put them there because they come in here and pay me
money to paint their portraits. And I do it – I take their
dirty money and paint those horrible men, even though
I think most of them should be charged with crimes
against humanity for what they've done, which doesn't say
a lot for me. But all of that – my venality included – is
the world, and I really don't want any more of it.'

'Golly, maybe you *do* need more time,' my mother said
laughing. 'But remember, I'm going to be sixty-eight on
my next birthday, and I don't *have* that much time. I'd
like a few years of not worrying about you. You probably
have no idea what it's like worrying about someone
twenty-four hours a day.'

I looked at her guiltily, but hesitated before I said
anything. 'No, I do actually,' I admitted at last. 'I remember
how it was after Gammy and Gabin died and before you
married Jasper – when you were living on your own down
the country. I had this worry about you all the time –
it never really went away. For me, the best part of your
marrying him was the way that worry just vanished.'

She was waiting for me to say more, but I stopped
then. I knew I should help her out, but I couldn't even
meet her eyes. Instead, I gazed down fixedly at the empty
cup and saucer I was holding, wishing I could put them
on the side table – just for something to do – but the
corset and the dress wouldn't let me stretch that far.

The idea that I was taking the fun out of my mother's
life – and I could see that maybe this was the case – was
one I didn't want to have to live with; but on the other
hand, I couldn't bear to think about changing my own life
either. Prolonged sickness probably never made anyone

unselfish, and I was no exception. I decided to change the subject.

'You know, I hate to say it, but it's probably about time I took off this dress. I want to pour us more tea, but it's so hard to move with this damn corset...'

'Oh, leave it on for another minute. I'll pour the tea. It's such a pleasure just looking at it.'

I stretched out a bit, to take some pressure off the diaphragm. 'I can't stop looking at it either,' I admitted. 'Anyway, wasn't last night...?'

'It really was. It was one of those times like...'

'Like my First Communion,' I said quickly. 'We'd been so miserable before it, hadn't we, and then the whole day was total fun. Just like last night. Do you remember how Aunt Betsy brought down Topsy and Charlie, and poor Topsy couldn't keep herself out of the cowpats, and we had to give her all those baths, and nearly a whole roast chicken, to keep her happy while we were doing it?'

'I do. I remember every bit of it,' she said laughing. 'Mainly I remember how it felt strange at the time – not quite right really – that we were enjoying ourselves so much.'

Neither of us said anything for a while, and then she surprised me by abruptly closing her eyes. I was reminded of how, in the first few years after my father died, any time I woke at night, I used to check that she was breathing.

'Are you all right?' I asked after a minute.

'Oh, I'm sorry, Maud. That must have looked odd to you. I suppose, it is odd, to be honest. I was just trying to remember for a moment how I felt the day your father had his accident, but I find I can't actually – which is interesting. In my brain, I know for certain it was the worst day of my life, but I can't recreate the feeling I had, the way I can recreate exactly how I felt the day of your Communion.'

'Well, for heaven's sake, stop trying. Maybe that means there's one good thing that can be said for the world after all – that bad stuff gets forgotten and nice stuff doesn't, so we can go on getting mileage out of it if we want to. Like my great party last night.'

'Or this dissolute morning after – the two of us waking up with mascara down to our cheekbones and nothing taken off but our high heels. And you in that gorgeous dress.'

The End

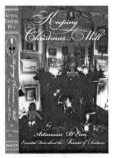

POVERTY IN IRELAND 1837
A Hungarian's View — Szegénység Irlandban
by Baron József EÖTVÖS 216 pages, 70 illustrations, bilingual

ISBNS (HBK): 9781908420206 (PBK): 9781908420213

THE STATE OF IRELAND AT THE END OF THE GEORGIAN PERIOD

Poverty in Ireland
1837
—*A Hungarian's View*—
Szegénység Irlandban

'This remarkable study of the causes and effects of poverty in pre-Famine Ireland was written by one of Hungary's first novelists and it's an acutely accurate account of conditions in the country in the mid-1830s. ... Phaeton has done an excellent job in creating this bilingual publication, with the Hungarian text on one side of the double pages and English on the other, all intermingled with an excellent series of period lithographs and a striking cover.' —*BOOKS IRELAND*

'There are few examples showing this troubled period of Ireland through the eyes of a foreigner (not Irish or British) with such scientific thoroughness and literary sensitivity. The book should be among the recommended readings for the responsible citizens of the European Union, as it brings forth information, patterns and morals about the history of our continent, about the roots of our present concerns. ... From a philological point of view, this is an exemplary edition, being the first annotated version of Eötvös's work ...'
— *CENTRAL EUROPEAN POLITICAL SCIENCE REVIEW*

PHAETON PUBLISHING LTD. DUBLIN WWW·PHAETON·IE

EXTREMELY ENTERTAINING SHORT STORIES
—Classic Works of a Master
by Stacy AUMONIER
576 pages: biography, 29 stories, & 1 essay
ISBNS (HBK): 9780955375651 (PBK): 9780955375637

STORIES OF WORLD WAR I & THE 1920S

'Stacy Aumonier is one of the best short story writers of all time.' —*JOHN GALSWORTHY* (winner of the Nobel Prize for Literature).

BROADCAST ON BBC RADIO 4 *Afternoon Readings*: '...not only hilarious, full of wit and genuine warmth for his subjects, but also beautifully constructed insights into the various absurdities of human behaviour...'—BBC *RADIO 4 PROGRAMMES*, 2011

'... a very elegant volume...short stories that invite comparison with those of Saki, O. Henry and even Guy de Maupassant.' —*BOOKS IRELAND*

'...in England...I bought the new Phaeton collection of *Extremely Entertaining Short Stories* by Stacy Aumonier ... Back now in New York, it's a heavy volume to cart back and forth as subway reading, but it's well worth the weight' —*LIBRARY JOURNAL*, NEW YORK

'Aumonier could condense a life into a few pages. ...unrivalled as a short story writer. ...Perfect with a hot toddy on a cold night.'–THE *INDEPENDENT*, LONDON

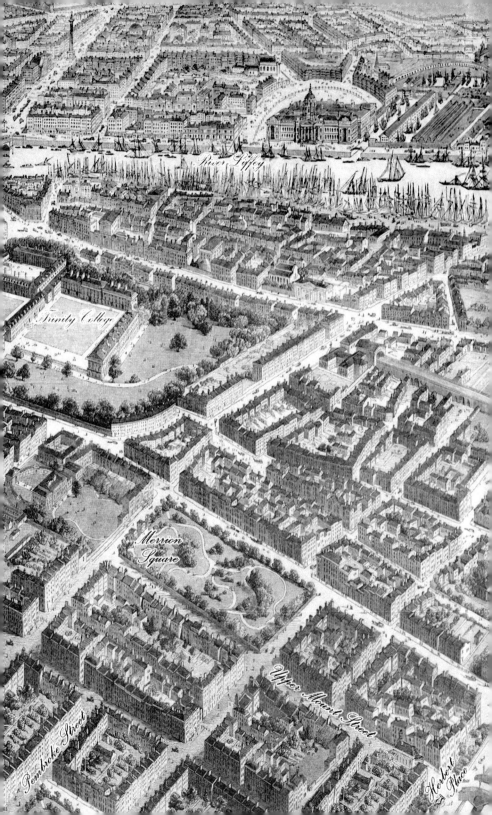

River Liffey

Trinity College

Merrion Square

Upper Mount Street

Pembroke Street

Herbert Place

CPSIA information can be obtained at www.ICGtesting.com
Printed in the USA
LVOW07*1453260916

506248LV00010B/63/P